Out

A car pulled up and [...]
driving. Jordan div[...]

"That was close," he said, out of breath. "Let's get away from here before they catch us."

Calley picked up speed. She pulled in and out of traffic.

"Watch it!" cried Jordan, as she narrowly missed a truck.

Calley quickly spun the wheel and swerved away. She weaved from side to side.

"Take it easy," said Jordan.

Calley turned sharply to the right and screeched around the corner. An empty wine bottle rolled out from under the seat. She tried to kick it back, but she couldn't quite reach it with her foot. She leaned down and frantically felt around the floor.

"Look out!" yelled Jordan.

But his warning was too late. Calley smashed into a telephone pole!

The Novels

NEW KIDS ON THE BLOCK™

Block Party

Seth McEvoy and Laure Smith

Boxtree

First published in the UK 1991
by BOXTREE LIMITED, 36 Tavistock Street, London
WC2E 7PB

First published as an Archway Paperback by POCKET BOOKS, a division of Simon & Schuster Inc. 1990

1 3 5 7 9 10 8 6 4 2

ISBN 1–85283–660–1

Printed and bound in Great Britain by Cox & Wyman Ltd., Reading, Berks.

Block Party

Chapter

1

"I'M ALL PACKED and ready to go on vacation," said Danny Wood. He lugged his overstuffed suitcase up to the front of the New Kids' tour bus and plopped down in the seat next to their manager, Dick Scott.

Dick glanced at his watch. "We'll be pulling into Boston in a few minutes. We should arrive right on time, bright and early at 8:10 in the morning."

"You're amazing," said Danny. "You have everything planned down to the last second."

"It's the only way I can keep track of all of

1

your concerts, interviews, and personal appearances," he explained.

Dick Scott did more than just keep track of details. The strong, confident man was always there for the New Kids whenever they needed him. No problem was too big or too small for Dick; he could handle anything. He was like a second father to them. "Danny, what have you got planned for your vacation?" he asked.

"I'm going to do something I haven't done since we started this concert tour."

Donnie Wahlberg leaned over the top of Danny's seat. "What's that?"

"Sleep!" Danny replied.

"No way—you're not," said Donnie. "We're headed for home. Whenever we make a pit stop in Boston, we have places to go, people to see, pizzas to conquer!"

Danny groaned and slid lower in his seat. He pulled his black hat over his eyes. "I think I'll get started on my sleep-a-thon right now. Wake me up in a week."

Jonathan Knight put his suitcases down beside Danny. "But what about the block party benefit concert we're giving for Dorchester Central High School? You can't miss that. Our families have planned the whole

"He smells like one, too!" added Jonathan.

Jordan grabbed a magazine off the floor and threw it at Danny. But Danny ducked to the side and it fell into Donnie's lap.

Donnie picked it up and flipped through the pages. "I don't believe it," he said, laughing out loud. "It says here in this tabloid magazine that I was kidnapped by aliens!"

"Why would aliens want you?" asked Danny.

"So I can teach them to sing and dance, of course. Haven't you heard that my amazing talent is known throughout the universe? It's a fact. It says it right here in black and white."

Danny laughed. "No, I hadn't heard that. Maybe I should read more tabloids so I can keep up with all the *facts.*"

"Listen to this!" Donnie exclaimed as he held up the magazine. "It says here that Jonathan is planning to have lots of children. And he's going to name them all after the Seven Dwarfs."

"Haawh! Haawh!" boomed Jonathan. "Last week they said I was going to name my kids after Santa's reindeer."

"That's a riot," said Danny. "I love all these wild things they say about us."

"Then you should listen to radio station

7

WTEA," said Mr. McIntyre. "They talk about you all the time. They have lots of news about what you're doing and where you're going. Fans call in and ask if the latest rumors are true."

"That sounds great," said Donnie. "I'd love to hear what our fans have to say."

Mr. McIntyre reached over and switched on the radio. The disc jockey's energetic voice blasted through the speaker. "This is Mad Jack McGee and it's time for the WTEA New Kids Hotline. We're coming to you from the heart of Boston with all the inside news and information on your favorite homeboys: Danny, Donnie, Jonathan, Jordan, and Joe!"

Joseph frowned at the radio. "My name is Joseph! Not Joe!"

"All you fans out there," said the D.J., "give us a call and tell us if you've spotted the New Kids in town yet. They should be arriving any minute. Here's our first caller: you're on the air!"

"Hi, I'm Erica and I love the New Kids. I've got their pictures all over my room, even on the floor and the ceiling."

"So, Erica, have you seen the fab five to-day?"

"Yeah! I just looked out my window and I

think I saw Jordan ride by on a skateboard. He had on a bright yellow T-shirt and lime-green shorts. But he had no hair. He must have shaved it all off."

Jordan ran his fingers through his thick brown hair. "No," he said. "It's still there."

Mad Jack came back on the radio. "Well, Erica, *that's* what WTEA wants to hear. Real news from real fans. Here's our next caller. You're on the air."

"I can't wait to see what this one says about us," Jonathan said eagerly. "Their enthusiasm is really amazing."

"We'd be nothing without our fans," Donnie added.

"Hi, I'm Rebecca from Jamaica Plain. I'm calling because I know that Jordan didn't shave his head. I just saw him at the 7-11 and—"

All of a sudden, Joseph yelled out, "Oh, no, look at all the girls in our yard! There are so many people you can barely see the house."

"Check out those banners and signs," said Donnie. "There must be hundreds of them."

"The Don't Go Girls made the signs," explained Mr. McIntyre.

"Who?" asked Danny.

"The Don't Go Girls," he said. "They're a

9

fan club named after your hit single, 'Please Don't Go, Girl.' They've been gathering around the house singing your songs ever since they heard you were coming home."

"I bet the neighbors aren't happy about that," said Joseph.

"They told me they don't mind," Mr. McIntyre replied. "Besides, it's only for a few days." He pulled on a red baseball cap that had the name LOBSTER LARRY stitched above the brim. "Everyone duck down," he said. "Then we'll drive right past them." When he drew closer, he honked the horn.

The fans immediately surrounded the van and screamed, "We want Joe! We want Joe!"

"He'll be here later," Mr. McIntyre said to them. "Let me through. I've got a delivery to make."

The girls cheered and slowly stepped back out of the way. He then drove through the crowd and around to the back of the house, where the New Kids safely ran inside.

The living room was packed with family and old friends. "Welcome home!" they all yelled.

"We're so glad to be here," said Donnie. "We really need a vacation."

"And this is the best place to have one,"

Jonathan added. "There's nothing better than coming home."

His mother, Marlene Putman, rushed over and gave him a big hug. "You look like you've lost weight."

"Oh, Mom, you always say that."

"Let's get some food in you. We've got plenty of it over on the dining room table. There's bacon and eggs, sausages and biscuits, and more!"

Jonathan kissed her on the cheek. "It's nice to see you're still worried about me."

"Hey, Danny," yelled his sister Melissa from across the room. "What's this I read about you? Are you really the reincarnation of Paul Revere?"

"No!" Danny grumbled. "It's just another silly rumor. Don't believe it."

Melissa laughed and gave her brother a hug. "But is it true that you fell off the stage and now you have psychic powers?"

"No, that's not true, either! I'm the same ol' Danny."

"Gee, that's too bad," joked Melissa. "I was hoping for a new and improved one that could read the future and tell my fortune."

Danny put his arm around her shoulder.

"You don't need me to tell you that. If you believe in yourself and work hard, your dreams will come true. Just like mine did."

"They sure have," she replied. "You New Kids never gave up. All that hard work you did, rehearsing every day after school for years, has really paid off. Now you can get me that present you promised me."

"What present?" asked Danny.

"You know. The big one you said you'd buy me someday if I didn't tell Mom about the time you—"

Danny suddenly interrupted her. "Now I remember. Don't say another word. I'll buy you anything you want, if you don't tell Mom."

Melissa had a twinkle in her eye when she said, "Yesterday I saw this silver Porsche that I liked a lot."

"You want a Porsche?" cried Danny. "Are you kidding?"

"Yes!" Melissa replied. "I'm just kidding. But I do need a new tube of toothpaste."

"I'll buy you a whole case. With fluoride!"

"That won't be necessary," she said. "One tube will do just fine."

Jordan was standing right behind her. He

turned around and looked puzzled. "What's this about a tuba? Is that Danny's latest plan to improve our act?"

"Maybe," Danny said mischievously. "Don't you think it would be great if I play the tuba, and you get a pair of bongo drums? Donnie and Jonathan and Joseph can each play an accordion."

"Don't say that too loud," said Jordan. "Someone might believe you and then we'll have another rumor on our hands."

Danny smiled. "Okay, I'll keep it quiet."

Donnie's sister Tracey handed Jonathan a glass of apple juice. "What's this I hear about you getting married to Madonna?" she asked.

Jonathan's laugh bellowed through the living room. "*Haawh! Haawh!* That's ridiculous. We're not even dating."

"So who are you going out with?"

"We're on the road so often, we don't have much time for dates."

"That's too bad," said Tracey. "I guess it's not always easy living the way you do."

"I'm not complaining," Jonathan replied. "I wouldn't trade my busy schedule for anything. Well . . . maybe world peace, or a chance to see a few Red Sox games."

Tracey smiled. "I hope it's okay that we've asked you to take time during your vacation to sing at the block party."

"Of course it is. We were all excited the minute we heard it was for Dorchester Central High School. We want to do everything we can so kids don't get hooked on drugs and alcohol."

Tracey put her empty glass down on the coffee table. "It's been hectic getting things organized. There's so much to do. We need to hire a few more people to sell tickets. But it's hard to find the right ones, because most of the people I've talked to aren't very responsible. If you know anyone who might be good, let us know."

"I will," he replied.

Over in the dining room, Jordan and Jonathan's sister, Allison, talked to Donnie. "Now that you're home, what are you looking forward to the most?"

"Finding the perfect bowl of baked beans. Nobody makes beans like Boston."

"Beans, yuk!" scowled Joseph, as he walked by with a tray of donuts. "I hate beans!"

"If beans are what you want," Allison said to Donnie, "then there's a new restaurant in town you'll love. It's called Just Beans."

"I'll be there first thing tomorrow."

"Did I hear that right?" asked Danny, coming up behind him. "Donnie Wahlberg is actually going to eat something nutritious? Run, call the WTEA hotline! This is earth-shattering news!"

"What are you talking about? I eat from the four major food groups every day: pizza, hamburgers, taco chips, and cola!"

The phone rang and Mr. McIntyre picked it up. He talked briefly, then called Joseph over. "It's Mr. Angelino from the deli."

"What does he want?"

Mr. McIntyre put his hand over the receiver. "He says you ordered ninety-eight dollars worth of deli food and had it delivered across town yesterday. Is that true?"

Joseph shook his head. "Of course not. It must be some mistake. We were traveling on the bus all night."

Mr. McIntyre explained that Joseph didn't order the food, but the deli owner wasn't convinced.

"Somebody must have made the order by pretending to be Joseph," said Sharon Knight, Jonathan and Jordan's sister.

"Someone pretending to be me?" asked Joseph.

"I bet Sharon's right," Jonathan agreed.

Joseph pulled at his father's arm. "Dad, tell Mr. Angelino that I'm coming over there to straighten this out. I'll be back in a few minutes."

"You mean *we'll* be back in a few minutes," said Donnie. "When there's trouble, the New Kids stick together."

Mr. McIntyre told Mr. Angelino that Joseph would be there soon. He hung up the phone and pulled out his car keys. "I'll take you over in Lobster Larry's van."

"Let me drive us there," asked Donnie. "I'm dying to get behind the wheel of that thing."

Mr. McIntyre tossed him the keys. "My friend Larry said you can use it all you want. But be careful; don't let the fans spot you."

"They won't!" Donnie assured him.

"Come on, guys," said Joseph. "Let's go see Mr. Angelino and take care of this mess."

Chapter
2

DONNIE PUT THE VAN in gear and pulled it around the side of the McIntyre house. In the front yard, the Don't Go Girls were all singing the New Kids' song "The Right Stuff."

"Donnie, you'd better put this on so no one will recognize you," said Joseph. He handed him the red fish-market cap his father had worn earlier.

Donnie pulled it on and honked the horn. The singing crowd moved aside without missing a note:

You got the right stuff, baby.
You're the reason why I sing this song.

"They sound pretty good," said Jordan. "Why don't we hire them as back-up singers?"

"Great idea," Danny replied. "I'd love to go on tour with a few hundred girls."

"We can't do that," said Joseph, cracking a smile. "They'd all fight over me."

Danny shoved him in the arm. "You mean they'd all fight to get *away* from you."

Joseph made a face at him.

Jonathan watched out the window as they drove through the streets of Boston. The narrow two-lane roads were jammed with cars darting in and out of traffic. Children played along the sidewalk in front of their houses. The two- and three-story buildings were all lined up close together, each one painted a different color.

People waved and shouted at the van when they drove by. "Hey, Lobster Larry," yelled a teenage boy. "How's it going?"

Donnie gave him the thumbs up, then he switched on the radio. "Let's see what else they're saying about us on WTEA."

". . . the New Kids were riding on top of a fire engine," said the young girl on the radio.

"Thanks for calling," the disc jockey replied. "That's the twenty-third New Kids' sighting we've had this morning. They must be running all over town. Our listeners have spotted them in Needham, Dedham, Wellesley, and Newton. And in Quincy, Braintree, Wakefield, and Peabody. Where will they turn up next? Here's another caller. Hi, you're on the air."

"My name is Cynthia and I live in Cambridge. My sister said she just saw Donnie in Harvard Square sitting on top of a statue of George Washington."

"Cynthia, I don't think there's a statue of George Washington in Harvard Square," answered the disc jockey.

"There's not? Well, maybe it was Benjamin Franklin."

"I don't think so," he added. "The Ben Franklin statue is on Park Street downtown. Let's see what our other listeners have to say. Hi, you're on the air."

"I'm Angela. Donnie couldn't have been in Harvard Square, because I just saw him water-skiing on the Charles River."

"Oh, really?" said the D.J. "Who else was with him?"

"I think Joseph was driving the boat but I'm not sure. He had on sunglasses."

"Thanks for calling, Angela. Get back to us if you see them again. Now it's time for the New Kids' Quiz. Our first question is about Jonathan. I want all you fans out there to call and tell us his middle name. If you get it right, you'll be eligible for our New Kids Super Quiz tomorrow. Here's our first caller."

"Is Jonathan's middle name Edgar?"

"No, sorry. Next caller."

"I think it's Sheldon."

"Wrong again. Next caller."

"That's an easy question. It's Rashleigh."

"You're right!" yelled the disc jockey. "What's your name?"

"Linda Beth."

"Okay, Linda Beth, see if you can answer this one and you'll win a giant New Kids' button. What's Jonathan's favorite laundry detergent?"

"Ah . . . um . . . Tide?"

"No, Linda Beth, you don't win the button, but you'll be eligible for our Super Quiz, so listen in for all the details."

"I will," she said.

"Now here's our next WTEA quiz question. Which New Kid wants to build a home in the shape of Big Bird?"

"I guess we'll never know the answer to that one," said Donnie, "because there's Angelino's up ahead." He pulled the van to a stop right in front of the two-story brick building. He flicked off the radio and everybody piled out.

Inside, small tables and wooden chairs filled the middle of the delicatessen. Three people were working behind the counter. Mr. Angelino's back was turned as he wrote the day's specials on the chalk board.

Joseph tapped him on the shoulder. "Excuse me."

"Ah, young Mr. McIntyre."

"I'm here to take care of this problem about the deli order. It's all a mistake."

Mr. Angelino wiped his hands on his white apron. "How can I be sure you didn't place that order?"

"Because we were on a bus last night, driving across New York and Connecticut."

"That's right," Jonathan added. "I was with him."

"But you could have called it in from any-where," said the deli owner.

"But I didn't," Joseph insisted.

"Somebody else must have pretended to be Joseph," Donnie explained.

"That may be true," replied Mr. Angelino. "But someone has to pay for that order or else I'll lose nearly a hundred dollars."

"The only way to solve this is to find out who really placed that order," said Jonathan. "What can you tell us about it? Maybe we can find a clue."

"You'll have to ask Calley Marvin. She's the one who answered the phone. Calley!"

"What is it?" asked the sixteen-year-old girl who shyly stepped out from behind the counter. Her long blond hair was tied up in a braid that ran halfway down her back.

"Tell Joseph about that order you took last night. I'll be in the basement, checking the bakery inventory."

Calley nodded. She nervously twisted her hair as she walked over. "Joseph, you don't remember me, do you?"

"Ah . . . ah . . . have we met before?"

"Yes, when I was six years old. We were in a play together at the children's theater."

Joseph snapped his fingers. "Now I remember. You played the little peasant girl."

"And you were my brother."

Jordan nudged Joseph in the arm. "Hey, why don't you introduce me to your *sister?*"

"Wait a minute, Romeo," said Joseph. "We've got to find out about this phony deli order. What can you tell us about it, Calley?"

"There's not much to tell. Some guy called up and ordered dozens of subs, sodas, and potato chips. He said to deliver them to 93 Perton Street. Then he hung up." Calley looked down and sighed. "The whole mix-up was all my fault. I should have called back to verify the order. I just . . ." She paused and struggled to say, "I just . . . forgot."

"Don't feel so bad about it," Joseph replied, reassuring her with a gentle pat on the shoulder. "We all make mistakes."

"But I . . . I can't afford to make one like this," she said. "I don't have the money to pay for it."

"What do you mean, pay for it?" asked Donnie.

"Mr. Angelino says that if the order was my mistake, then I have to pay for it because I forgot to call back and check up on it."

"That's terrible," said Jordan. "Don't worry. We'll find out who did it. We won't let you take the blame."

"But I don't have any idea who it might have been."

"Maybe we can find out," said Jonathan. "Where did you say the order was delivered to?"

"93 Perton Street."

Jonathan pulled out a little notebook and wrote it down. "Where's that?"

"It's in a neighborhood across town," said Donnie.

"Who delivered the order?" asked Danny.

Calley pointed to a dark-haired teenager sweeping the floor. "Mr. Angelino's nephew, Frankie, made the delivery."

"Maybe he can help us," said Joseph.

Calley called him over.

"What do you want?" he asked.

"Can you tell us about the delivery you made to Perton Street last night?" asked Joseph.

"There's not much to tell," Frankie replied. "I took all the stuff over there, just like I was supposed to."

"Who was there to pick it up?"

"I didn't see anybody. I knocked on the

door, and someone called down and said to leave the food out on the porch. I did and then I left. That's it."

"What time did you make the delivery?"

"About ten o'clock."

Jonathan turned to Calley. "What time did the order come in?"

"Nine o'clock," she replied.

"That doesn't tell us much," he said. "The only clue we've got is the address. We should go over there and check it out right away."

"If you don't find anything," Calley replied, "I'll have to come up with a way to pay Mr. Angelino."

"You won't have to," Joseph insisted. "We'll all pitch in and help pay."

Calley shook her head. "It's really nice of you to offer, but this mistake is my fault and it's my responsibility to take care of it. I don't know how I'm going to come up with that much money, but I'll find a way. Maybe I'll get a second job."

"I know how you can make some money," said Jonathan. "Tracey Wahlberg told me that she wanted to hire an assistant to help with the block party."

"What block party?" asked Calley.

"The one that our families are organizing to

raise money for the high school," he explained. "Haven't you heard about it?"

"No. I guess not."

"I'll have one of our sisters call you," said Jonathan. "She'll tell you all the details."

"I'll do anything to pay back Mr. Angelino," Calley promised. "Tell her I'll work really hard and do whatever she needs."

"That'll be great," Jonathan replied. "Now let's go check out that address."

Donnie straightened his cap. "I'm ready to roll."

"We'll keep you posted," Joseph told Calley as he and the others headed for the door.

Donnie cautiously looked outside and checked both directions. "It's all clear. No fans in sight."

Everyone rushed out, jumped in Lobster Larry's van, and took off.

When they drove away, Calley asked Frankie, "Will you watch the counter for me while I take my break?"

"Sure," he said. "But don't take too long. I've got deliveries to make."

"No problem," she replied. Calley grabbed her backpack and rushed into a tiny room in the rear of the deli. It was barely bigger than a broom closet. She closed the door and switched the lock in place. She checked it twice before she pulled out a small bottle of wine. Her hands fumbled as she tore off the top. Calley drank down two gulps and leaned back against the wall. "Now that's better," she muttered, and then took another drink.

Donnie slowed the van and turned onto Perton Street. Most of the old brick row houses were boarded up and abandoned, condemned to be torn down. Only a few were still occupied. A fat man in an undershirt looked down from a third floor window.

"This sure is a deserted neighborhood," Jonathan grumbled.

"There's number 93," said Joseph, pointing to the left. "I don't think anyone lives there anymore, because it has plywood on all the windows."

A cat ran in front of the van and Donnie slammed on the brakes, just in time. "Let's check out this place."

The New Kids climbed the staircase. The cracked cement crumbled away with every step. A huge NO TRESPASSING sign was stapled to the front door. It said, VIOLATORS WILL BE PROSECUTED.

27

Donnie peered through a crack in the door. "There's nothing inside. Nobody lives here."

"But what about the deli food?" asked Joseph.

"There's no sign of it," Donnie replied.

"Maybe we should ask the neighbors," suggested Danny.

Donnie glanced around. The fat man was gone from the window and there was no one in sight. "What neighbors? Even if we did find somebody, I don't think the people who live here would tell us anything. Let's go!"

The New Kids were disappointed they didn't find any clues, but they were relieved to get back into the van and speed away.

Donnie switched on the radio just as the D.J. said, "This is the Boston WTEA Party bringing you more New Kids news than any other station. Keep listening for the latest updates. We'll be bringing you the inside information on who they are, where they are, and what they're doing. Our next program is the Dream Date show. Call up and tell us what you'd like to do on a date with your favorite New Kid. Here's our first caller. What's your name?"

"I'm Mindy and I'd love to go on a date with

Joseph. I'd like to take him to Lincoln, Nebraska, because that's where I used to live and there's this great hot dog place there where we can eat foot-long hot dogs with chili and relish on top. . . ."

Donnie's eyes lit up. "That sounds like my kind of date. I love hot dogs!"

"Thanks for calling," said the disc jockey. "Who's next?"

"My name is Kayla and I want to go out with Danny more than anything in the world. He's so cute and I love the way the edges of his mouth turn up when he smiles."

"Where do you want to go on a date with Danny?" asked the D.J.

"I read that he has an ant farm and he loves to watch all the ants run around inside. So I'd like to go over to his house and watch the ant farm, too. Maybe he'd even name one of the ants after me."

"Now *that's* a dream date!" the D.J. shouted into the microphone. "I certainly hope it comes true."

Danny laughed. "I don't have an ant farm. Where did she hear that?"

Donnie pointed to the radio. "Probably right here on WTEA."

"Is this the station that's interviewing us

tomorrow?" asked Jordan. "Sharon said we were scheduled to go to one of the radio stations to talk about the block party concert."

"It's this one," said Jonathan. "I love their call-in shows."

"Hey, listen to this," yelled Donnie as he turned up the volume on the radio.

"Oh, yes, Donnie's my favorite because he's cute and smart and strong and talented and funny and kind and he likes stuffed animals."

"That's me!" Donnie said proudly.

"He's also friendly, honest, loyal, and trustworthy."

"He sounds like a Saint Bernard," Joseph joked. "Woof! Woof!"

"Don't laugh," Donnie replied. "This girl's smart. She knows what she's talking about. I want to hear more." He turned the volume up even louder.

". . . but if I can't go out with Donnie, I guess I'll go out with Jonathan. As a matter of fact, I like him better anyway. He's so cute and smart and strong and . . ."

Donnie immediately turned off the radio and everyone burst out laughing. He then drove up to the McIntyres' and through the crowd.

When they went inside everybody wanted to

know what was going on. Jonathan explained what had happened. After he told them about Calley and their trip to Perton Street, the phone rang.

Mr. McIntyre answered it. He looked worried as he spoke into the receiver. When he hung up, he asked Danny, "Didn't you tell me that your brother Brett is out of town this week visiting friends?"

"That's right. Why, is something wrong?"

"I think so. That was Waldo's Record Store on the phone. Someone at your house told him you were over here. Waldo says that Brett Wood just called in an order of records and charged them to Danny. He says Brett is coming by to pick them up in a few minutes."

"It must be another impostor," Danny replied. "First Joseph and now me!"

"I'll call him right back and cancel the order," said Mr. McIntyre.

"Wait!" said Donnie. "Don't call him. I've got an idea! Let's go over there and catch this jerk red-handed!"

Mr. McIntyre looked concerned. "I don't think that's a good idea. There could be trouble. Why don't I call Waldo and let him take care of it?"

"If you call him, he might accidentally scare off the impostors," Donnie explained. "Then we may never find out who's doing this to us."

"You may be right," Mr. McIntyre agreed. "Okay, go see what you can do."

Chapter

3

DONNIE PULLED THE VAN up alongside Waldo's Record Store. Danny was the first one to jump out. When he raced for the store, a car horn blasted behind him. He turned to look and ran smack into a customer walking out the door. Records flew into the air and scattered across the sidewalk.

"I'm really sorry!" Danny said as he reached down to help pick them up. "If anything's broken, I'll . . ." Before he could finish his sentence, the customer scooped up the records and hurried away.

The New Kids entered the store, and Danny

asked to see Waldo. The short, bearded man said he was Waldo and Danny introduced himself. "Somebody claiming to be my brother, Brett, is going to pick up an order of records. Could you point him out when he gets here?"

"I can't," said Waldo.

"But he's an impostor! My brother is out of town."

"I can't point him out because he just left with a big stack of records."

"Was he wearing a blue Boston Celtics sweatshirt?" asked Danny.

Waldo nodded. "Yes, and a big pair of sunglasses."

"I'm going after him," Danny declared. He ran outside and was halfway down the street before the other New Kids left the store.

Up ahead he spotted someone wearing a blue sweatshirt. He had the hood pulled up over his hair. The person turned and saw Danny racing toward him and immediately darted between two buildings.

When Danny reached the alley, there was no one in sight. Joseph, Donnie, Jonathan, and Jordan ran up beside him as he waved down a boy on a skateboard. "Did you see someone in a Celtics sweatshirt go through here?"

"He was carrying a big stack of records," Joseph added.

The boy flipped his skateboard up into the air. "Yeah, I saw him."

"Which way did he go?" Danny asked.

The boy pointed across the street to the Franklin Park Zoo.

"We'll never find him in there!" groaned Jonathan.

"Sure we will!" said Donnie. "Let's go!"

The New Kids rushed over to the entrance and hurried inside. The seventy-acre park was packed with children running in every direction. Jonathan and Jordan searched through the monkey house, and Donnie and Joseph raced past the aviary and the waterfowl pond. But they didn't see anything. Danny ran across the entire length of the Children's Zoo, looking everywhere, but he didn't have any luck, either.

"There isn't one single blue Celtics sweatshirt in this whole place," he said to Donnie as he sat down on a garbage can shaped like a baby elephant. "I think we lost him."

"Or her," added Jordan. "We don't know for sure if it was a boy or a girl."

"I guess not," said Danny. "Maybe it was a girl. I couldn't see a face. It looks like we've hit

35

another dead end. Why don't we head back to Joseph's place?"

Just as they turned to leave, a young girl screamed, "JORDAN! It's Jordan Knight. It's really you. Jordan! Yowee!"

Donnie held his finger to his lips. "*Sssh!!* Don't let anyone know we're here," he told her. "Or we'll never get out of the zoo in one piece."

"Okay, sure," she said, talking softly, but even faster. "Wow, I don't believe it. It's all five of you. Shauna will just die when I tell her I saw the New Kids. She's your biggest fan. No, *I'm* your biggest fan. I've got all your records and posters and T-shirts and everything."

"Would you like an autograph?" asked Jordan.

The girl's mouth dropped open as she nodded her head.

Jonathan pulled a piece of paper out of his pocket and everyone signed it. She didn't reply when Donnie said they had to leave. She just stared right at him and silently watched while they left the zoo, the paper gripped tightly in her hand.

The New Kids barely managed to get home without being mobbed. A group of girls recognized them as they drove through the neighborhood, but they were able to pull into Joseph's without any trouble.

As soon as they came in the house, Sharon asked, "Did you catch the impostor?"

"No," Danny answered. "We chased him into the zoo and he got away."

"Or her," Jordan added.

"Tell those policemen what happened," Sharon said, motioning across the room. A burly red-headed officer was munching on a jelly donut. Another one was talking to Melissa Wood. When the five singers walked up beside the two men, the red-headed one asked, "Are you the New Kids?"

"That's right," said Donnie.

"I'm Officer Breen," he replied. "This is Officer Bradley. Waldo called the station about the impostor at his store. Ms. Wood told me there's been a similar incident at Angelino's Deli. What do you know about this?"

The New Kids told them every detail and Officer Breen asked, "Are you sure this isn't a publicity stunt?"

"Of course not!" Donnie answered angrily.

"We'd never do anything like that!" said Joseph.

"I'm not so sure," grumbled Officer Breen.

37

"I've heard that you show business types will do anything for publicity."

"No way!" protested Jonathan. "We wouldn't want the media to hear about this. It might give other people ideas!"

"I see your point," said Officer Bradley. "We'll look into the situation and see what we can find out."

"Thanks," said Jonathan.

On his way out the door, Officer Bradley turned and said, "We'll keep you informed if we discover anything."

Donnie squeezed an orange in his hands. "I don't know how that Breen guy could think we pulled those stunts for publicity. We've got so much publicity we could bottle it and sell it to starving third-world rock bands."

"We've got to find out what's going on," said Jonathan. "But we don't have any clues."

"I just remembered something about the stolen records," said Danny.

"What's that?" asked Jonathan.

"All the records were by heavy metal groups! So maybe the impostor is a heavy metal fan."

"I have a friend who plays in a heavy metal band," said Donnie. "Maybe he can help us. His group is called the Ironheads. Last I heard, they were playing around town."

"Who is this guy?" asked Danny.

"Do you remember Bruno Nadler?"

"Yeah, he was in my fifth grade math class. Let's go see him."

The five singers climbed into the lobster van and drove off again. Minutes later they pulled up in front of Bruno's two-story wooden-frame house. Donnie and the others ran up the front steps and rang the bell.

A teenage boy in a black leather jacket opened the door. His long brown hair fell down around his shoulders. He broke into a smile when he saw Donnie. "It's Wahlberg the Wildman! How ya doin'?"

"Not too bad," he replied. "I just stopped by to ask you a couple of questions."

"Sure, come on in," said Bruno, swinging open the screen door so everyone could come inside.

"You know all the guys, don't you?" asked Donnie.

Bruno nodded. "Jonathan and Jordan and I were in the church choir together," he said. "And Danny and I used to make the biggest snowmen in the neighborhood. But I've never met Joseph."

"Glad to know you," said Joseph, stepping forward to shake hands.

39

"Is it true that you're quitting the band to become a lion tamer?" Bruno asked him.

"No. And I'm not the long-lost son of Elvis, either."

"Really?" Danny said jokingly. "I thought that rumor was true."

Joseph didn't answer. He just shook his head and groaned.

"Why don't we go to the basement," Bruno suggested. "The band's down there practicing."

"I've heard about your band," said Jordan. "My cousin told me you were great. He said that someday you'll be bigger than Aerosmith."

"I hope so," Bruno replied as he climbed down the steps.

The huge basement had dozens of heavy metal posters plastered across the walls. Musical equipment was scattered everywhere.

"We've got company," Bruno said to the two teenage boys sitting on the beat-up old couch. "This is Donnie, Danny, Jonathan, Jordan, and Joseph."

"You mean, the New Kids on the Block?" asked the short, muscular boy.

"That's right, Jerry," replied Bruno. He

introduced everyone to Jerry Glass, the keyboard player, and Tim Fong, the drummer.

"I remember you, Danny," said Tim, sliding a drumstick through his fingers. "But all I ever saw of you was the back of your head."

Danny looked puzzled. "Where was this? Did you sit behind me in class?"

"No," Tim answered. "You always beat me in track."

"Now I remember. How are you doing?"

"Not too bad, but not as good as you."

"Why not?" asked Danny.

"Your band's a big hit and ours is still just playing local clubs."

"You'll make it," said Donnie. "Just keep practicing. It took us years to make it."

"He's right," said Jonathan. "They practically threw us off the stage the first time we played in public."

"No kiddin'?" Jerry replied.

Donnie then explained about the impostor who had taken all the heavy metal records. "Do you know anybody who might have done something like that?" he asked.

"I'm not sure," said Bruno. "But I'll look into it. We know almost every heavy metal fan in town."

41

"Thanks a lot," Donnie said to him with a smile. "We'd better be moving on. Our families threw us this big welcome-home party over at Joseph's and we haven't been there for more than ten minutes. All we've been doing is running around Boston trying to straighten out this mess. So we'll see you guys later."

Inside the van, Jonathan asked if anyone else noticed the left-over deli food on the table down in Bruno's basement.

Jordan nodded. "Yeah, I saw it. There were bags and napkins that said ANGELINO'S in big black letters."

"Do you think they could have placed that phony deli order?" asked Danny.

"No way!" Donnie protested as he started up the van. "They'd never do anything like that."

"We can't be sure," Joseph added. "They could be the ones who took those heavy metal records, too!"

"I'll never believe it," said Donnie. "I've known Bruno for years."

"But then who's pulling these stunts?" asked Joseph.

"Could it be Calley?" Danny suggested.

"That's not very likely," said Jonathan. "Look how she wanted to pay for her mistakes, all by herself. If she had placed that deli order, I bet she would have jumped at our offer to help pay."

"You may be right," said Danny. He let out a big yawn. "I sure am tired. We've been driving around so much I feel like we're still on tour. I could use a few hours sleep."

"Coming right up," said Donnie, pressing down on the gas pedal. "You're on your way home right now."

Donnie drove the van through the crowd at the Woods' house and let Danny off at the rear door. When he pulled back out into the street, he switched on the radio. "I wonder what's happening on ol' WTEA?"

"Give us a call," said the disc jockey, "and tell us what you think about this New Kids feud we've been hearing so much about."

"What feud?" asked Jonathan.

"I don't know," Donnie replied. "I haven't heard anything about a feud. Let's see what they have to say about it on the radio."

"Here's our next caller," said the D.J. "You're on the air."

"Hi, my name is Julie and I think it's

43

terrible that Joseph won't let Donnie wear orange socks. I can understand why Donnie is so mad at him. It's not fair; he should be able to wear whatever he wants."

"I agree," the D.J. replied. "Freedom of footwear is a birthright of all Americans. Here's our next caller. What do you have to say about this?"

"Well, I think it's just awful that Jordan is on Joseph's side. Jordan used to be my favorite, but now I like Donnie better. I'm going to knit him a pair of orange socks. I don't care if Joseph and Jordan think they're ugly."

"Thanks for giving us your opinion. Here's our next caller."

"My name is Patty and I'm so upset that the New Kids are fighting over Donnie's orange socks. Jordan shouldn't have flushed them down the toilet. My friend Sheila told me that Jonathan's really mad at Jordan and won't even talk to him. That's really sad. I heard they were going to break up over this."

All of a sudden, Donnie stopped the van and jumped out. He ran over to a phone booth and dialed the radio station.

The disc jockey immediately interrupted the caller on the air. "Listen, up all you New

Kids fans out there, we've got Donnie
Wahlberg on the line. So, Donnie, what's all
this we hear about a feud over socks?"

"Don't believe a word of it," said Donnie.
"All the New Kids love my orange socks."

"That's good news!" cried the D.J. "We've
had hundreds of calls. Everyone has been
concerned about this."

"There's no need to worry," Donnie replied.
"We're getting along great. We plan on singing
together forever. Someday we may have to
change our name to the Old Men on the Block,
but we'll still have the 'right stuff.'"

"So tell us, Donnie," said the disc jockey.
"Where are you calling from?"

"Ah . . . Anchorage, Alaska."

"Come on, Donnie. Tell us where you are.
You've got thousands of fans out there who
want to know."

"The only thing I'll tell you is that I'm not
anywhere near Plymouth Rock."

"That's bad news for all the girls down there
in Plymouth. But good news for everyone else,
because one of your fans might be lucky
enough to cross your path."

"I have to be taking off," said Donnie.

"We'll be looking forward to hearing more

from you tomorrow when you and the other New Kids come into the station for a WTEA exclusive interview."

"We'll be there," Donnie promised. He hung up the phone, climbed into the van, and rushed back to the McIntyres'.

When Donnie, Joseph, Jonathan, and Jordan went inside, they were happy to find that everyone was still there talking, eating, and having a good time.

Sharon waved to Jonathan. She brought him a cheese danish and asked, "What was the name of that girl you said could help out with the block party?"

"Calley Marvin," he replied. "She works at Angelino's Deli."

"I'll go over there and set up the details," she said. "Then I'll see you guys at home later."

As Sharon headed to the deli, she had no way of knowing that she had driven right past Calley, who was on her way to the liquor store.

Calley nervously entered the store and edged up to the front counter, where a young man was working the cash register. She gave him a twenty-dollar bill and asked for the cheapest bottle of wine in the store.

46

He wrapped the bottle in a paper sack and handed it to her.

"Where's my change?" asked Calley.

"Extra charges," he answered. "You're under age."

"Please don't tell anyone."

"No problem; your secret's safe with me!"

Chapter

4

THE NEXT MORNING at the Knights' house, Jonathan and Jordan had a late breakfast with Sharon, Allison, and their mother.

"Where's Nikko?" asked Jonathan. "Come here, boy. Come get something to eat."

The big, friendly Sharpei bounded into the kitchen. The dog's wrinkled coat hung so loosely on his body that it looked as if his skin was three sizes too big.

Jonathan scratched Nikko under the chin. "I hope your ear infection is all cleared up."

Sharon handed Jonathan a buttered bagel. "The vet says he's just fine, but don't let him go into a swimming pool for a while or it might come back."

"That's too bad," said Jonathan. "Nikko just loves to jump off the diving board."

"Yeah," Jordan grumbled. "And every time he does, he climbs out of the pool, runs over to me, and shakes himself dry."

Jonathan laughed. "He must think you need a shower."

Jordan scowled at him. The phone rang and he picked it up. "Hello? Calley? How ya doin'? . . . Oh, I'm so glad. That mix-up with the deli order was terrible. We've been trying to find out who did it, but we haven't had any luck . . . You don't have to thank me. I wanted to help . . . Oh, sure, she's here. Hey, Sharon, Calley got your message. She wants to talk to you about the block party."

Jordan handed her the phone, then said to Nikko, "So you think I need a shower?"

The dog tipped his head to the side.

"You'd better not come near me when I wash Mom's car this afternoon, or you'll be the one who gets all wet this time."

Nikko grabbed Jordan's shoelace between his teeth and jerked it to the side.

"Hey, let go!" cried Jordan as he struggled to pull it out of the dog's mouth.

Nikko tugged at the shoelace even harder, and all of a sudden, Jordan fell over backwards.

"Yikes!" he yelled, his arms flying up over his head.

Splat! Jordan landed right in Nikko's water dish.

"*Haawh! Haawh!*" Jonathan bellowed. "It looks like Nikko just showed you who's boss."

Jordan stood up and inspected his jeans. They were soaking wet. "Look what he did. These pants are brand new."

"Oh, they'll be fine," said his mother. "Just put them in the washing machine. I've already got a load of dark clothes in there."

Jordan grumbled under his breath as he left the room.

Sharon hung up the phone and Allison cleared away the breakfast dishes while their mother wrote a grocery list.

"That dog of yours is pretty smart," said Sharon.

"He sure is," Jonathan proudly replied. "I've taught him a lot of tricks, and they've come in handy. One time we were trapped in an elevator with a dozen fans. They wouldn't open the door and let us out. I signaled for Nikko to start sneezing and they immediately

50

ran away. Another time when fans were chasing us down the streets of Sacramento, I told Nikko to begin limping. All of a sudden, the girls stopped to find out what was wrong with him. As soon as we were safely back at the tour bus, he quit pretending to be hurt and raced after us."

"He's amazing," said Allison.

"He's a menace!" added Jordan as he came into the room in a dry pair of jeans.

"Don't say that too loud," Jonathan warned, "or I'll have him show you his extra-special trick."

"What's that?" asked Jordan.

"Are you sure you want to know?"

"Ah . . . well . . . maybe not."

The phone rang again. This time Sharon answered it. "T-shirts? I don't know anything about that." She put her hand over the receiver and turned to Allison. "Did you order another box of T-shirts for the block party?"

Allison shook her head. "No, I didn't. I picked up twenty boxes yesterday. That's all we need. We won't sell more than that."

"I don't understand what's going on," Sharon said. "Somebody ordered an extra box from Casey's T-shirt shop yesterday. When they came by to pick them up this morning, they said to charge them to our account. Casey is calling to make sure the address is correct."

Jonathan stood up from the table. "This sounds like those two incidents yesterday. Tell Casey we'll come by and straighten it out."

"I'll go with you," said Allison. "Sharon has some business to take care of."

When Sharon hung up the phone, Jonathan asked, "What T-shirts is he talking about?"

"I'll show you." She reached into a cardboard box on top of the refrigerator. She held up a big black T-shirt. It had pictures of all five New Kids on the front. On the back it said THE BLOCK PARTY in dayglow yellow letters. "We're going to sell these at the concert tomorrow."

"Why would somebody order an extra box?" asked Jordan.

"Who knows?" answered Sharon. "They might want them for themselves, or maybe they want to sell them and keep the money."

"Or possibly they want them as collector's items," added Allison. "These T-shirts are going to be valuable someday."

"That's right," Sharon agreed. "Everything you guys touch becomes a collector's item. You wouldn't believe some of the offers I've had for your old stuff."

"Remember that guy who came by a couple

of weeks ago?" their mother asked. "He wanted to pay me a thousand dollars for Jordan's old tricycle. So who knows what those T-shirts could be worth?"

"Maybe Tracey Wahlberg knows something about this," said Allison. "I took a few boxes over to her house yesterday. I'll give her a call." Allison talked to her briefly and then hung up the phone. "She doesn't know anything about an extra order either."

Jonathan looked worried as he stood up from the table. "We've got to find out who's ripping us off."

"How do we know it's one person?" asked Jordan. "Maybe it's just three unrelated incidents."

"That's possible," agreed Jonathan. "I wish we had more clues. It might be the Ironheads, but it could be anyone."

"Maybe the police have come up with something," suggested Sharon.

"They told us that they would keep us posted," said Jonathan. "But I don't think Officer Breen really believes there is an impostor."

"Or two or three," Jordan added.

"It looks like the only thing we can do is investigate this problem ourselves," replied

Jonathan. "So let's posse up and ride on over to the T-shirt shop."

Allison peeked out the window. "There's still an army of fans out front. You'll never make it past them. We'll have to find a way to sneak you out of here."

"Why don't we hide in the trunk of your car?" suggested Jonathan. "It won't be the first time we've had to do that."

Jordan frowned at the idea. "Do you still have that bag full of smelly old gym clothes in there?"

Allison laughed. "No, I finally took that out. Now all I keep in the trunk is garlic, onions, and Limburger cheese."

Jordan gripped his stomach, pretending to be sick. "I wonder who it was that invented sisters?"

"I'm only kidding, Jordan. The trunk is clean and empty and ready for passengers. Let's go."

Jonathan and Jordan kissed Sharon and their mother good-bye. They went out the back door and climbed into the trunk of Allison's car. When she drove down the driveway, a fan raced up to her. "Where's Jonathan and Jordan?"

"Inside," Allison replied.

"I hope they come out soon! I traveled all the way from Rhode Island to see them."

"Maybe they will," she answered as she pulled out into the street. "The boys are inside all right—inside my trunk."

Casey's T-shirt Shop was only a few blocks away. Allison parked the car on a deserted side street. She cautiously lifted the trunk lid and her brothers hopped out.

"I thought you'd never get here," Jonathan grumbled. "It was awful!"

"What was awful?" asked Allison.

"Being cooped up with Jordan! When we hit a bump in the road, he suddenly had a great idea for a song. He tapped out the beat on the lid of the trunk and then sang at the top of his lungs. I'm almost deaf."

"But it's a great song," Jordan protested.

Allison tugged at Jonathan's arm. "Come on, you guys, let's get inside. Someone might see you."

They hurried into the small T-shirt shop. Its racks were packed full of shirts in every size, shape, and color. Dozens of belts, buttons, and hats hung on the racks behind the cash register.

"What can I do for you?" inquired a slim young man wearing a Bruce Springsteen T-shirt.

"Are you Casey?" asked Allison.

"That's right."

"You talked to my sister Sharon . . ."

"You must be Allison," Casey said with a big wide smile. "And you're Jonathan and Jordan," he added. "All of our New Kids T-shirts sell like crazy."

"I'm glad to hear it," said Jonathan. "We came by to find out about that order of T-shirts you called about earlier."

"The order was phoned in yesterday," said Casey. "A boy came by and picked them up first thing this morning. He said to charge them to the Knights' account."

"Can you remember anything else?" asked Jonathan. "What did he look like?"

"Now that I think about it, I don't know. He had on a big old raincoat and a wide-brim hat that came down over his eyes. I couldn't see his face."

"If you couldn't see his face," asked Jordan, "are you sure it was a boy?"

"No, I guess I'm not really sure. It might have been a girl. I couldn't tell by the voice because he or she only mumbled a few words."

Jonathan let out a discouraged sigh. "This is getting worse and worse by the minute. We don't have a single clue and now we'll have to pay for a whole box of T-shirts."

"No you don't," said Casey. "I've decided to donate the twenty-one boxes to the block party benefit concert. That way all the money raised by selling them can go directly toward the drug and alcohol program at the high school."

"Thanks a lot!" said Allison. "I really appreciate your making such a generous contribution."

"So do I," Jonathan added.

Jordan reached out to shake Casey's hand. "Me, too," he said.

Allison pulled her keys out of her purse. "It looks like we've done all we can here, so I'm going to run over to Angelino's Deli. Sharon asked me to take some benefit tickets to Calley so she can start selling them. Do you guys want me to run you back home?"

"We'll go with you," said Jonathan. "I'll call Danny, Donnie, and Joseph, and have them meet us there. They'll want to hear all about this problem with the T-shirts right away. Besides, we've got a radio interview this afternoon and then we can go over there together."

"You are welcome to use my phone," said Casey, pulling it out from under the counter.

"Thanks," Jonathan replied.

As he called the others, Jordan wandered over to the front window of the T-shirt shop. His eyes lit up when he spotted a group of girls outside wearing black block party T-shirts. "Hey, Allison, come here."

"What's going on?" she asked.

"Look at those girls at the bus stop," he said.

"Is that all you ever think about . . . girls?"

"Look at them," he insisted. "They're wearing our block party T-shirts. Didn't Sharon say they weren't going to sell them until the concert tomorrow?"

"Maybe Casey knows something about this," suggested Allison. "I'll go ask."

She returned a minute later. "No, he said he never sold any. I wonder where they got them?"

"I'm going to follow those girls and find out."

"You can't. Someone will recognize you and you'll be mobbed."

Jordan thought for a moment, then he spotted the hats for sale. "Go buy me one of those baseball caps."

"What?"

"Please? The bus may come any minute. And get one for Jonathan, too."

"Oh, okay. I might as well try to stop a hurricane."

When Jonathan came over, Jordan explained his plan. Allison quickly bought two hats and gave them to her brothers.

"I can't wear this," complained Jordan. "It says, I LOVE DONNIE."

"You think yours is bad, look at mine! It says, KISS ME, I'M PREGNANT."

Jordan reluctantly put on his hat. "When you get to Angelino's," he said to Allison, "tell the guys we'll be there soon."

"I will."

Just as she drove away, Jordan spotted a bus coming. "Let's go see what we can find out."

The Knights raced out the door, but before they could get across the street, the crowd of girls screamed, "Jonathan! Jordan!"

"Oh, no," cried Jordan. "We'd better get out of here as fast as we can."

The two brothers took off running, but the girls were right behind them!

"Where's Nikko when I need him?" Jonathan joked as they raced around a corner.

"What are we going to do now?" asked Jordan, glancing over his shoulder.

"There's a 'T' station near here some-where," said Jonathan.

The two brothers ran to the right and dodged around another corner. "There it is!" shouted Jonathan.

Jordan looked back. The girls were half a block away. He and Jonathan flew into the subway station and ran to the toll booth. Jordan fumbled through his pockets and pulled out a handful of change. He plopped it all down on the counter. "We want two to-kens."

"Here come the girls!" yelled Jonathan. "Let's move."

They grabbed up their tokens and rushed to the turnstile. The train roared into the station and screeched to a stop. The doors flew open and Jordan and Jonathan jumped inside.

The screaming pack of girls charged toward the door . . . but it slammed shut just before they got there.

"That was close," Jordan said with a sigh of relief.

Chapter
5

AFTER JONATHAN AND JORDAN arrived at Angelino's Deli, they huddled together with the other New Kids at a table in the corner. There were four other customers in the store, but fortunately no one recognized them.

Over at the deli counter, Allison gave Calley block party tickets and fliers. She waved goodbye to everyone and hurried off to take care of more business.

Frankie Angelino brought a tray full of food over to the New Kids. "Who ordered the meatball sub?" he asked.

"I did," Donnie replied.

"Who's having the ham and cheese on rye bread with horseradish and double mustard?"

"That's mine, too."

"And what about this triple-decker tuna sandwich, whose is that?"

"Put it here," said Donnie.

"Are these two orders of potato salad also yours?"

"No way! What do you think I am, some kind of pig?"

"Don't mind him," said Danny. "He gets real cranky when he hasn't eaten in over an hour."

Frankie laughed. He set the sodas down on the table and pulled a paper napkin out of the metal holder. "Could I have your autograph?" he asked, holding out the napkin.

"Sure, no problem," Donnie replied. He scribbled down his name and the others signed theirs alongside it.

"Thanks!" said Frankie. "I'm so glad I got your autograph before you guys broke up the band."

"What are you talking about?" asked Danny. "We're not splitting up."

"Well, I read that you guys were going to quit singing and move to Texas to become astronauts."

"Then we'd be the New Kids on the Moon," joked Donnie.

"No, Frankie," said Jonathan, "we're not quitting the band or moving anywhere. How could we leave good old Beantown? This is our home."

"Beans!" Donnie exclaimed. "Do you serve baked beans here?"

"Coming right up," Frankie replied.

"Make it a *double* order!"

As Donnie shoveled down his food, Jordan explained more about the girls he and Jonathan had seen wearing block party T-shirts. "They might be the impostors," he said. "Those girls could have placed the phony orders because they probably know lots of personal details about us. Most of our fans do."

"That's right," said Joseph. "They even know how many fillings I have."

"You have fillings?" asked Danny. "I thought you had false teeth."

"No way," Joseph protested. "I've still got my natural-born teeth. All the better to bite you with!" He leaned over and took hold of Danny's shirt.

"Hey, Joseph," said Jordan. "If you're that hungry, I'll order you a hamburger."

Joseph let go of Danny's shirt and playfully growled at Jordan.

Jonathan didn't even notice them because he was so lost in thought. "I hate to admit it," he said, "but the impostor could be one of our fans."

"I think it might be the Ironheads," said Danny. "We saw the deli wrappers at Bruno's and we know they like heavy metal."

"Maybe those girls like heavy metal, too," suggested Joseph.

Danny shook his head. "Most of our fans don't like heavy metal."

"How do you know that?" asked Donnie.

"It said so in a magazine."

"Well, then it *must* be true," Donnie said sarcastically. "Because everything they print about us is true, right?"

Danny looked embarrassed. "No," he said, "of course not!"

Joseph set down his empty soda can and Calley came over to clear the table. "If those girls had stolen the T-shirts," he said, "they wouldn't have been wearing them right across the street from where they just stole them."

"We're getting nowhere," Jonathan said with a frustrated sigh. "It's almost time to go to the radio station for our interview."

"It's at WTEA, right?" asked Joseph.

"Yeah," Jonathan replied. "They're on the other side of town."

"I'm going with you," said Calley. "Allison asked if I would go there to sell tickets and hand out fliers to the crowd. There will be hundreds of your fans at the station."

"I'm glad you're coming," said Jordan.

Calley blushed bright red.

"By the way," he asked the others, "how are we getting there?"

Donnie held up a set of car keys. "We've got Lobster Larry's limousine service."

"Not again!" Jordan groaned.

"That's right," said Donnie. "Let's move on outta here."

Just as they were almost to the door, Frankie yelled, "Stop! You can't take the van."

"Why not?" asked Donnie.

"I was listening to WTEA on the radio and they just announced that you guys are driving it around town."

"Oh, no!" Jonathan groaned. "How are we going to get to the interview now?"

"Maybe we could reschedule it," Joseph suggested.

Donnie shook his head. "No, we can't. They've been advertising that we'll be there, and besides, we need to tell everyone about the benefit concert tomorrow."

"I'll drive you to the station," said Frankie. "You can hide in the back of our delivery truck." He held up a handful of white aprons and paper hats. "Wear these and you can sneak inside pretending to make a delivery. I'll go get some cardboard boxes for you to carry."

"I think Frankie's plan will work," Donnie told everyone.

"Let's do it!" replied Joseph.

The New Kids tied on the aprons and put on the hats. They each grabbed a box and loaded into Angelino's delivery truck with Calley and Frankie.

When they pulled out into the street, Donnie realized that they should hide the lobster van. He drove it into the garage behind the deli and raced back toward the truck. Just before he got there, two girls wearing New Kids T-shirts screamed out, "Donnie! Donnie!"

He ran even faster and dived into the back just as Frankie pulled away from the curb.

"That was close!" he exclaimed, climbing up on one of the benches.

"What if those fans call the radio station

and tell everyone we're in here?" asked Jonathan.

"There's not much we can do about it now," Donnie replied.

"Why don't we listen to the radio and see what's happening over there?" suggested Danny.

"Good idea," Jonathan answered.

He tuned in WTEA just as the disc jockey said, "Get ready, all you New Kids fans. Your favorite boys from Boston will be here in less than ten minutes. We'll be playing all their hits until they arrive. So stay tuned for the big event. Our first song will be one of my favorites, 'Cover Girl.'"

When the song started, Jonathan turned the volume down a little bit and Frankie sped through the narrow twisting roads of Boston. He darted around a rotary and headed along a tree-lined street. In the back, Calley pulled the block party fliers out of her backpack. She nervously flipped through the pages, then straightened them over and over again.

Jordan noticed that she seemed fidgety. "What's wrong, Calley?" he asked.

"Oh . . . ah . . . I'm just . . . thirsty."

"Why don't you take a drink of my soda," he said, handing her the can.

"Oh . . . oh, thanks." She nervously took a drink from the can and handed it back, not daring to admit that what she really wanted was a drink from the bottle of wine in her backpack.

Jordan smiled at her, then said to Danny, "I just can't get those girls out of my mind."

"What girls?" he asked.

"The ones who were wearing those block party T-shirts that we saw earlier today. I can't prove it, but I have this feeling that those T-shirts are a big clue."

"What did the girls look like?" asked Calley. "Maybe I know them."

"There must have been a dozen or so," he said. "But I remember that one of them had bright red hair with a streak of green on one side."

"Did she wear glasses?" asked Calley. "Big black ones?"

"Yeah."

"That's Mary Ann Lewis. She's president of the Don't Go Girls Fan Club."

Joseph snapped his fingers. "I saw her outside my house yesterday. She was carrying a big sign with Jonathan's picture on it."

"That's her, all right," said Calley. "She's

crazy about him. She'd do anything to get closer to him."

Jonathan looked worried. "Anything? Even place a phony T-shirt order?"

"Maybe," Calley answered.

"We'd better investigate these Don't Go Girls some more."

Calley noticed Jordan looking at her as she fingered her long blond braid. "I hope you make it through the crowd without getting hurt," she said to him.

"Don't worry," he replied. "We do things like this a lot. It usually works out okay."

"Most of the time," Jonathan added. "Remember what happened in Madrid?"

"What?" Calley asked anxiously.

"You promised you wouldn't tell anyone about that," Jordan protested.

Jonathan cracked a smile. "I don't remember saying that."

"Oh, Jonathan, please tell me what happened," begged Calley.

"Don't you dare!" yelled Jordan. "It's too embarrassing."

All of a sudden, Frankie jerked the truck to the right. Everyone slid across to the other side. Jordan bumped up against Calley. They both were surprised and smiled shyly at each other.

"What's going on?" Donnie asked Frankie.

"I just remembered that this alley will take us around to the back of the radio station. Now you won't have to go in the front way. You can safely sneak inside the rear entrance. See! There's no one in sight."

"Nice going," said Danny, as they pulled to a stop.

Frankie jumped out and knocked on the door. A guard opened it and motioned for the New Kids to come inside. They threw off their aprons and paper hats. Frankie told them he had a delivery to make and that he would be right back to pick them up.

As they headed into the building, they could hear the crowd outside singing their song, "Step by Step."

When they stopped at the elevator, Calley said, "I'll see you guys later. I'm going out the front door."

Jordan blew her a kiss. She blushed as she waved back.

"So what's the deal, little brother?" asked Jonathan.

Jordan didn't answer as he watched Calley

walk away. The elevator opened and Jonathan pushed him into it.

"When's the wedding?" asked Joseph, pressing the third floor button.

Jordan didn't say a word the rest of the way up.

When the elevator came to a stop, Donnie exclaimed, "This is it! Now it's time for us to go to work."

The New Kids stepped into the reception area of WTEA. A nervous young assistant ran up to them. "You're going on the air in thirty seconds. Follow me." They all rushed down the hall and squeezed into a tiny room full of electronic equipment.

"And here they are now," said the disc jockey into one of the microphones. "This is Mad Jack McGee bringing you live and in person the New Kids on the Block! What's all this I hear about you? Does Donnie really have a wooden leg? Is Joe going to star in a movie with Pee Wee Herman? Is it true that Jonathan and Jordan are twins? And what about Danny? Does he really eat seaweed ice cream?"

The New Kids were crowded around the other microphone. Jordan tried to answer, but he couldn't stop laughing, so Donnie leaned over and said, "The answers to your questions are: no, no, no, and yes!"

"That's what your fans want to know," Jack yelled into the microphone. "So who's going to be the first New Kid to get married?"

Everyone pointed to Jordan. He turned as red as a beet.

"So it's Jordan!" cried Jack. "When's the big day?"

"Ah . . . um . . . " he stammered. "June first, 1999."

The disc jockey turned to Joseph. "What about you, Joe? When are you getting married?"

"Twenty or thirty years from now."

"Don't let Joseph fool you," said Donnie. "He's been married six times already. But each wife ran away because he played his Frank Sinatra records all day."

Joseph grabbed the microphone and leaned into it. "Don't believe a word he says. I've never been married. But I want to someday."

"And she'd better like Frank Sinatra," said Jonathan. "Because he listens to his records *all* the time."

"That's true," Joseph replied. "Frank's the greatest."

"He sure is," said Mad Jack. "And he's got blue eyes just like our pal Joe here. Maybe they're related?"

"No such luck," Joseph answered.

"Too bad," said the D.J. "Now tell us about this benefit concert you're giving tomorrow."

Danny explained that it was to raise money for the Drug and Alcohol Rehabilitation Center at Dorchester Central High School.

The disc jockey congratulated the New Kids on all the anti-drug and anti-alcohol work they had been doing, then he said, "Now it's time for the New Kids Super Quiz. All you fans out there who've answered one of our daily quizzes are eligible to call in and talk to your favorite singer in person. If you can guess the weight of one of the New Kids, you'll win a personally autographed poster. We've got five of them. One for each correct answer."

At that moment the production assistant carried a big scale into the control booth. She had five posters rolled up under her arm. She laid them out on the table for the New Kids to sign.

Mad Jack told the radio audience that Danny was to be the first one on the scale. The phone lines lit up and he took the first caller.

"Hi, my name is Edna and I just love Danny. I know everything about him."

"So, Edna," the D.J. said. "How much does he weigh?"

"162 pounds," she said. They all were surprised when they looked down at the scale.

"That's right," Jack replied. "You win a poster and get the chance to talk to Danny. Here he is!"

"Hello, Edna," said Danny. "How are you doin'?"

"I'm . . . I'm . . . fine," she said nervously. "Is it true that you just bought a 1960 red Buick Skylark with a black interior and white-wall tires?" she asked.

"No, that's not true. Where did you hear that?"

"My cousin Angel told me. She said she saw you driving it in Sacramento."

"No, Edna, I don't have a car yet. I'm not sure what kind I'd buy. I might like something made the year I was born, 1970."

"What color?" she asked.

"Dayglow orange."

"That's my favorite color," she replied.

"Me, too."

"Well, Edna, your time's up," said Mad Jack. "Come down to the station and pick up your prize. Now I want all you fans out there to guess Jonathan's weight. Give us a call with your answers. Hi, you're on the air."

"My name's Pamela, and I read that Jonathan weighs 155 pounds."

"Let's see if that's right," said the D.J.

Jonathan stepped up onto the scale. He shook his head.

"Sorry, Pammy, but that's not the right answer. Here's our next caller."

"Does he weigh 112 pounds?" asked the young girl.

"No way," exclaimed Jack. "Why did you pick that number?"

"Because that's how much I weigh," she replied. "And I was hoping we had something in common."

"You both listen to the fabulous Boston WTEA party," said the D.J. "You have that in common. Thanks for calling. Hello, you're on the air."

"Hi, I'm Renée and I've read everything about Jonathan. I know he likes Italian food and sailing and scuba diving and his favorite show is 'This Old House.' I also know that he's a Sagittarius with hazel eyes and brown—"

The D.J. suddenly cut her off. "That's great, Renée, but how much does he weigh?"

"I read that he loses weight on tour and I know he's been touring for a long time now, so my guess is 151 pounds."

"That's correct!" yelled Jack. "You win the poster and here's Jonathan."

"Hi, Renée," Jonathan said into the microphone. "That was a good guess. How did you know I lose weight on tour?"

"My neighbor's stepsister's cousin has an uncle who's a hairdresser of the aunt twice removed to your nephew's teacher's father. His plumber told me."

"He's right," Jonathan replied. "When we're on tour, my mom's always calling me up and asking what I ate that day. She thinks I'm too thin."

"Oh, no you're not," said Renée. "You're just right. No, you're perfect."

"That's not what Jordan says," Jonathan told her. "He thinks I talk too much, snore too loud, and have awful taste in shoes."

"Well, he's wrong and I'll tell him so if I ever see him. He shouldn't pick on your snoring. That's not fair! I'm going to write him a letter. He should be nice to you. I'm sure you're a great brother and a great human being. They should make you president."

"If I'm president," said Jonathan, "I won't have time to sing with the New Kids."

"Oh, that would be terrible," Renée replied. "Then they should make you vice president. That way you'd have lots of free time."

The D.J. interrupted and told Renée that her time was up. He then asked everyone to call in and guess the weight of the other three New Kids. They guessed Donnie and Jordan right away, but it took ten calls before anybody got Joseph's weight right.

When the interview was over, the New Kids headed back out to the reception area, where a program assistant handed Donnie a telephone message.

"Oh, no," he exclaimed. "Frankie can't come to pick us up. How are we going to get out of here?"

Chapter

6

OUTSIDE THE RADIO STATION, Calley squeezed her way through the crowd. Everyone was singing New Kids songs and chanting the name of his or her favorite band member. She passed out all of the block party fliers and then started selling the concert tickets. Hundreds of fans eagerly bought them as fast as she could sell them.

She sold the last one and slowly inched her way to the edge of the crowd, where she was surprised to see three teenage boys shouting at a police officer. His name badge read OFFICER BREEN.

Calley recognized the boys immediately.

They were the Ironheads. Bruno and Tim used to come into Angelino's Deli all the time, but they hadn't been in for weeks.

Bruno yelled at the policeman, "We're the Ironheads and we want to see the New Kids."

"We've got something for them," said Tim, shaking his drumsticks. "Let us in!"

Calley stepped back into the crowd when Jerry got angry and tried to push his way past Officer Breen. The policeman grabbed Jerry by the shoulder and squeezed as hard as he could. "Don't even think of taking another step, punk. Now get out of here before I run you in."

"Hey, that's police brutality!" shouted Tim. "You can't shove us around."

"Keep your mouth shut or I'll take you in for questioning!"

"On what charge?" asked Bruno.

"Harassing the New Kids," said the officer, staring him straight in the eyes. "I have a report that somebody's been impersonating them."

"Not us!" Jerry snapped back.

"Then get out of here!" yelled Breen. "Right now."

"But we've got to see the New Kids!" Bruno insisted. "It's important."

79

"You heard what I said," the policeman snarled. "If you're not out of here in ten seconds, I'm taking you down to headquarters."

"Okay," grumbled Bruno. "But you're making a big mistake!" He turned and angrily stormed off with Jerry and Tim right behind him.

As Calley watched them leave, she wondered if Danny might be right. Maybe the Ironheads had been impersonating the New Kids, she thought. If they haven't been into Angelino's lately, then how come they had all those deli sandwiches? "I think I'd better follow them and see what I can find out," she said to herself.

In the lobby at the radio station, Joseph picked up the phone and dialed home. It rang and rang, but no one answered. "There's nobody there," he said. "I'm surprised. There is always someone home."

"Why don't I try my house?" suggested Danny.

"No," Donnie replied. "I've got a better idea. See that telephone truck down there?"

Danny leaned over to the window. "The one with the cherry-picker-type crane on the top?"

"Yeah!" Donnie answered. "I'll call the phone company and see if they can drive it under the window. Then they can raise that crane up and lift us out of here in the cherry picker compartment."

"All of us can't get into that little thing," said Jonathan. "We're too heavy."

"Sure we can," Donnie replied confidently. "My friend's father works for the phone company. He says those cranes can carry up to two thousand pounds. They use them to lift heavy transformers, so they have to be strong. I'll call my friend's father."

In less than ten minutes, the phone truck moved across the street toward the radio station.

Donnie opened the window and yelled, "Bring it over here!"

The truck slowly made its way through the fans below. When it reached the side of the building, the cherry picker crane was raised up to the window. A man from the phone company climbed through the window and told everyone what to do.

"It'll be a tight squeeze, but we can all fit inside," said Donnie. He eagerly made his way into the open compartment.

The other New Kids squeezed in after him

81

and the phone company employee signalled down to the driver.

The driver turned on his loudspeaker and asked everyone to move aside. The truck slowly edged back and pulled away from the building. The fans yelled out for the New Kids. All five waved to the crowd. The fans cheered even louder.

The New Kids held on tight as they moved through the air.

Donnie waved at a young woman in a third floor office as they rode by. The woman was so surprised she dropped an armload of papers all over the floor.

Danny grinned as they turned the corner. "This is even better than that time in New Orleans when we had to climb out onto a fire truck. They just lifted us onto another building so we could get into our tour bus. This time we get to ride down the street."

"I asked one of those firemen if we could jump into their emergency net," said Joseph. "They said we could the next time we're in town. I can't wait."

The phone truck came to a stop a mile away and the driver lowered the crane to the ground. "How did you like the ride?" he asked.

"It was better than a roller coaster!" said

Donnie as he hopped out onto the side-walk.

"Thanks a lot," added Jonathan.

The driver smiled. "My daughter, Erin, is a big New Kids fan. She'll be excited to hear that I met you. Could I get your autographs?"

"Sure," said Danny. He pulled a block party flier out of his pocket and wrote a short note to Erin. Jonathan, Jordan, Joseph, and Donnie all added a few words.

"Thanks, guys. My daughter will love this."

Calley followed the Ironheads to the nearest T entrance. She hung back out of sight as they went inside and bought three tokens. When Bruno led the others through the turnstile, Calley took a token out of her pocket and cautiously went in after them.

The subway train came to a stop and the Ironheads got into the first car. Calley rushed over to the second one. She nervously hung on to one of the overhead handles as the train pulled out of the station.

Each time the train stopped she poked her head out the door to see if the Ironheads were getting off. Finally, at the fourth stop, the teenagers jumped out the door and raced up the stairs. Calley ran after them.

She climbed out onto the street and looked around. Up ahead, she saw Bruno and the others go around the corner. She shivered when she realized that she was in a deserted part of town. Calley reached inside her backpack and pulled out a small bottle of red wine. She took a long drink and immediately felt better. She then stuffed the empty bottle into her jacket pocket and hurried after the Ironheads.

Calley snuck around the corner and saw them pry open a boarded-up window in front of an abandoned red brick building. The band members disappeared inside.

"It's the same address!" she said to herself. "93 Perton Street. That's where Frankie delivered the phony deli order."

The street was almost empty except for an old woman sitting in the window of a nearby building. Calley ignored her as she crept up to the crumbling building. It had a NO TRESPASSING sign posted on each of the boarded-up windows. In big red letters it said, VIOLATORS WILL BE PROSECUTED.

Without making a sound, Calley stepped onto a pile of wooden boxes and reached for the fire escape ladder. She easily pulled herself up onto it. "Good thing I spent all those years taking gymnastics," she said under her breath.

Calley silently climbed to the third floor. She stopped cold when she heard voices through the boarded-up window.

"How are we going to get to the New Kids?" asked Jerry. "They're surrounded by mobs of fans everywhere they go."

Calley's heart pounded. She didn't know what the Ironheads would do if they discovered she was outside. Calley tried to calm her fears, but she couldn't stand the tension. Her fingers reached for the bottle in her pocket. One drink would calm her down, she thought.

She leaned closer to hear what they were saying and suddenly her hand slipped. The bottle slid out of her pocket and fell to the pavement below. CRASH! It shattered into a million pieces.

The old woman yelled out the window. "Hey, what's going on over there? I'm calling the cops!"

Calley quickly scrambled up the fire escape. She reached the roof just as Bruno pushed away the board and poked his head outside.

"See anything?" asked Tim.

Bruno shook his head. "No, but I'm sure

someone was here." He shoved the board farther to get a better look. RRRIIP! The board tore free and tumbled off the side of the building. It smashed onto the street just as a police car pulled up. Two officers jumped out.

"The cops are coming!" yelled Bruno. "Get out of here, quick!"

The Ironheads scrambled through the building and flew out the back door.

Calley peered over the edge of the roof. When she saw the police climbing up the fire escape, she panicked. The sign on the building had said that trespassers would be prosecuted and she didn't want to get caught. She frantically ran across the roof and searched for an exit. The door to the stairs was locked. The other buildings were too far away, so she didn't dare try to jump. There was no other way out but back down the fire escape.

Calley cautiously peered over the edge of the building again and saw the police climb through an open window. They were inside for only a few minutes before they came back out to the fire escape. She could barely hear what they were saying.

"Didn't you tell me that Breen and Bradley were working on a New Kids case?" asked a policewoman.

"Yeah," answered the male officer. "Maybe they'd like to take a look at all these T-shirts. They might be a clue."

Each cop carried an armload of black T-shirts down to the patrol car. Calley recognized the block party design from the fliers.

When the police were gone, Calley climbed down and ran to the MTA station as fast as she could. She knew that the New Kids would be eager to hear what she had discovered.

The train arrived right away and Calley sat down in the first car. She nervously bit her lip as the subway car twisted and turned through the dark tunnel. She reached into her backpack and felt around for a bottle of wine. "Oh, no," she muttered to herself. "I'm all out."

Chapter
7

THE NEXT MORNING, when Jordan and his sister
Sharon went to Angelino's Deli, Calley rushed
up to meet them. "I think I know who's been
impersonating the New Kids."

"Who is it?" asked Sharon.

"The Ironheads!" Calley exclaimed. She
then told them everything that had happened
the day before. Everything except the part
about the wine.

When she was finished, Jordan pulled out
one of the deli chairs and sat down. "Why
didn't you call someone about this last night?"

Calley froze. She couldn't tell him that she'd

had too much to drink and that she had fallen asleep. She didn't know what to say.

"Ah . . . I . . . I tried to call," she began. "But . . . ah . . . the lines were busy."

"I'm not surprised," Jordan replied. "All of us have such big families that the phones and the bathrooms are often busy twenty-four hours a day. You should have tried to come by."

"Well . . . ah . . . there are hundreds of girls surrounding your houses. I didn't think I'd ever get through."

"You're probably right," Jordan agreed.

"Besides," Calley went on, "I knew I could tell Sharon about it this morning, because she was planning to come by and pick up the ticket money."

"Did you call the police and tell them what you found out?" asked Sharon.

"No, not yet," Calley replied. "I . . . I . . . wasn't sure who to call or what to say. I thought I should talk to one of the New Kids first."

"I know who to call," said Jordan. "Can we use that pay phone over there?"

Calley nodded and followed him over to it.

Jordan spoke to Officer Breen and explained what had happened. He then called the other

New Kids and told them the same story. When he hung up the phone, he said, "Everyone should be here in a few minutes."

Sharon paid Mr. Angelino for an apple. She bit into it as she walked beside her brother. "How much ticket money have you collected?" she asked Calley. "If you give it to me, I'll take it to the bank."

Calley panicked when she remembered that she'd bought two bottles of wine with some of the money. She didn't know how she was going to explain what had happened to it. She thought fast, then pretended to dig into her pocket, looking for it. "Oh, no," she said, trying to sound surprised. "I left it at home. It's sitting on the dresser in the bedroom."

"No problem," said Sharon. "I can get it another time. I've got some errands to run, so I'll see you guys later. Bye."

As soon as she left, Frankie ran into the deli. "Hey, guess what happened?"

"What?" asked Jordan.

"Somebody stole one of the raffle prizes for the New Kids block party!"

"Which one?"

"Danny's charcoal drawing of Boston Harbor."

"How did it happen?"

90

"When I was over at the Dorchester Central High School making a delivery to the decorating committee," Frankie began, "I noticed a weird-looking girl leaving the room where the prizes were kept. Two minutes later, one of the committee members yelled that somebody had stolen Danny's drawing."

"That's terrible," said Calley. "Who was the girl?"

"I don't know."

"What did she look like?" asked Jordan. "You said she was weird looking."

"She had long red hair with a green streak on the side. And she wore these big black glasses that were really ugly."

"Mary Ann Lewis!" cried Calley. "The leader of the Don't Go Girls."

"I'm getting really suspicious of them," said Jordan. "We should find out more about that club."

"I still think it's the Ironheads," Calley replied.

"We don't have enough evidence to prove anything," said Jordan. "It could be either one."

Just then, Danny raced into the deli. Donnie was right behind him.

"This whole situation is getting out of

hand," said Donnie. "We've got to do something before it gets worse."

Joseph looked discouraged when he came through the door.

Danny asked him why.

"I was just talking to Officer Breen on the phone," he said. "He still thinks all these incidents are some kind of publicity stunt. That man has a real attitude problem."

Jonathan arrived a few minutes later. His shirt was torn and his hair was messed up.

Donnie was surprised to see him look so sloppy. He was always so neat and organized. "What happened to you?"

"Don't ask!" Jonathan replied, running his fingers through his hair. Jordan told everyone about the stolen drawing and Calley repeated what had happened with the Ironheads. Frankie brought everyone sodas as the New Kids debated about who was guilty.

Joseph leaned back in his chair. "I think the evidence points to the Ironheads. They had the deli food and they like heavy metal. The biggest clue is that our T-shirts were found in their hideout."

Donnie disagreed. "Anyone could have planted them there."

"That's possible," said Joseph. "But it's so

hard for me to believe our fans could have done all those things."

"But what about the drawing?" asked Jonathan. "Who else would want it but a fan?"

"This keeps getting more and more confusing," said Danny.

"I think we should find out more about these Don't Go Girls," said Jordan.

"But how?" asked Joseph. "We can't just go up and talk to them."

Donnie's eyes lit up. "Maybe we can if we disguise ourselves."

"As what?" asked Jonathan.

"We could dress up as New Kids' fans and try to join their club," Donnie suggested.

"No way," protested Jordan. "I'm not going to wear girls' clothes."

Donnie thought for a moment. "Well ... then why don't we disguise ourselves as punk rockers? I could put blue food coloring in my hair and wear my dad's old black raincoat."

Jonathan looked doubtful. "Remember that time you dyed your hair green for St. Patrick's Day? It didn't come out for a week."

"Then I'll wear a wig."

"I've got an idea," said Calley. "This spring the high school drama department put on the play, *Grease*. I bet you could use their black

93

leather jackets and long wigs to dress up as a heavy metal band."

"I like that idea," said Danny.

"Me, too," added Joseph.

"Do you think we can use their costumes?" asked Donnie.

"I know the drama coach," said Calley. "I'll call him and ask if you can come over."

"Thanks," said Jordan, giving her a big smile.

Jonathan grimaced. "Why do I let myself get talked into these schemes?"

"Because they work!" Donnie replied.

"Oh, yeah?" said Jonathan. "What about that time in Denver when we put on gorilla suits and they dragged us off to the zoo?"

Donnie shrugged his shoulders. "How was I to know the zippers would get stuck?"

"And what about Miami? You said no one would recognize us if we wore those football uniforms."

"It almost worked," said Donnie, shrugging his shoulders.

"But your plan backfired when a car pulled up with our music blasting out the window. Jordan started dancing and we were spotted right away. A hundred girls chased us down the street and into the ocean!"

"Well," Donnie replied, "you said you wanted to go swimming."

"I'd rather wear my bathing suit."

"You're so fussy, Jonathan."

Calley ran over and said the drama coach was glad to help the New Kids in an emergency. "I wish I didn't have to work this morning because I'd love to see you guys dressed up as a heavy metal band."

"We'll take pictures for you," promised Joseph. "I've got my pocket camera."

"You're not going to take *my* picture," said Jonathan. "You'll probably send it into a fan magazine."

"Who, me?" Joseph asked, trying to look innocent. "Would I do that?"

"Yes!" everyone replied.

The New Kids drove over to the high school in Donnie's mother's car. They headed into the costume department and pulled the black leather jackets off the racks.

Danny picked out a sleeveless white T-shirt and a long blond wig. He struggled to put on the wig, but it kept falling off. "How do I keep this thing in place?" he asked.

"Try using a hammer and nails," said Jonathan. "Your head's hard enough."

"So is yours," he snapped back. "Because it's full of rocks."

"Rocks and roll!" Jonathan jokingly replied.

Joseph groaned. "If you're going to tell jokes like that, then we'll all start telling terrible puns."

Jordan tossed a long black wig at Joseph. He caught it with one hand and put it on. "I've got a great idea," he said. "We could all wear black and white nuns' habits and call ourselves The Singing Nuns."

"Why don't we get giant hot dog costumes?" suggested Jonathan. "Then we'll be The Dancing Buns."

"Yeah!" Joseph exclaimed. "Or we could dress up as the ex-President and First Lady, and we'd be The Reaganites."

"If you two don't stop," said Donnie, "you'll both be pushing up roses."

Joseph turned to Jonathan. "I don't think he likes our jokes."

"That's because they're not funny!" Donnie said as he pulled up his black jeans and put on a big studded belt.

"Sure they are," Joseph replied. "That's why we should call our heavy metal band Puns R Us."

"I give up!" said Donnie, shaking his head. "We've created a monster."

Joseph tied a bandana around his wig and went on and on with more silly names: "Gumbies 'N' Hoses, Bubblegum 'N' Noses, Sons 'N' Glozes, and Bleeguns 'N' Plozes."

"What's Bleeguns 'N' Plozes?" asked Danny.

Joseph shrugged his shoulders.

Danny started to laugh just as Donnie asked if everyone was ready.

"I am," yelled Joseph. Then he jumped up on a chair and snapped everyone's picture.

"Give me that camera," yelled Jordan. He ran across the room and chased Joseph down the hall.

Joseph hopped onto a table and Jordan grabbed for the camera.

"I got it!" He turned the camera and took two shots of Joseph. "I'm going to send *your* picture to every fan magazine in the country."

Chapter

8

"WHERE ARE WE GOING to meet the Don't Go Girls?" Jonathan asked Donnie.

"Calley said that they'll be either at one of our houses or over in Boston Common."

"Why don't we try the park first," said Jonathan.

"Good idea," Donnie replied. "Let's go!"

Danny still couldn't keep his wig on as Donnie drove over to Boston Common, the fifty-acre park in the center of town. The tree-covered common was crowded with people walking, jogging, and sitting on the grass.

Donnie parked the car on a side street and everyone headed into the park.

"When I was little," said Danny, "I used to come over here and play Frisbee. My brother and I would stay for hours. I just love this place."

"I flew my first kite here," said Joseph. "I think it got caught in that tree over there."

"Look!" Jordan pointed into the crowd. "There's a girl with long red hair and a green streak on the side. I think those other girls with her are the ones we saw outside Casey's T-shirt shop. Yeah, I remember those two on the right."

"Do you remember every girl you've ever seen?" asked Danny.

"Of course," he replied. "What's more important than that?"

"Okay, guys, are you ready?" Donnie asked everyone.

Jonathan straightened his black leather jacket and pulled a few strands of his dark wig over his eyes. "I guess I am."

Jordan zipped his jacket halfway up. He didn't have a shirt on underneath. A set of silver chains hung down across his bare chest.

Donnie led the way. His black pants were so tight he had to take short little steps. "Excuse me," he said to Mary Ann. "Are you a New Kids' fan?"

"Of course," she said. "I love the New Kids. We all do. We're in the Don't Go Girls Fan Club and we're going to their block party concert tonight."

"So are we," said Jordan. "We're big fans of theirs."

"You are?" asked Mary Ann.

"Oh, yeah," Jonathan replied from under his wig. "We've known them all our lives."

"We know them better than we know ourselves," added Jordan.

"Who's your favorite?" asked a girl in a long white New Kids T-shirt.

"I don't know," Jordan replied. "I can't decide. Who's your favorite?"

"Mine is Joseph," she answered. "I read that he's the smartest."

"No way!" Danny protested. "That's not what I heard. He doesn't even know how to tie his own shoelaces."

Her mouth dropped open. "Really?"

Danny held up his right hand. "I swear on the New Kids' first album."

Joseph pushed Danny aside. "Don't listen to

him. He doesn't know anything about Joseph, but I do . . . I'm his best friend."

The girl eagerly grabbed him by the arm. "So is it true what they say about him? Does he like girls with tattoos?"

Joseph tried not to laugh, but he couldn't stop himself. He cracked up and walked away.

"What's wrong?" asked the girl.

"Don't worry about him," said Jonathan. "He's got this little problem. He bursts out laughing for no reason. We try to ignore it. You should, too."

"Oh," said the girl. "I understand."

"You know what I just heard about Danny?" asked Mary Ann.

Danny bristled. "What?"

"He wears dance tights under his costumes."

"Why?" said one of the other girls.

"He thinks it makes him dance better; it's something about spinning faster."

"My sister told me she saw Jordan yesterday," added another girl, "and he had shaved his head! Well, whatever they're into . . ."

"That sounds gross," said a short girl with black hair. "But you know what? I read the New Kids' next album is going to be all country music!"

"Is that right?" asked Donnie.

"Oh, yeah," replied the girl. "I heard that they're all moving to Nashville onto a big farm where they'll raise goats and pigs. Or is it cows and chickens?"

"Penguins," Donnie said sarcastically. "They're going to raise penguins."

"That's cool," said a freckle-faced girl. "I love penguins. I've got a big stuffed one right next to my giant poster of the New Kids."

"Where did you buy your poster?" asked Donnie.

"I got a special deal when I joined the Don't Go Girls. They had them for sale at half price."

"Do you think we could join?" he asked.

Mary Ann looked surprised. "You want to join our fan club?"

"Yeah," Donnie replied.

"But it's an all-girl club. That's why we're called the Don't Go Girls."

"Then we'll call ourselves the Don't Go *Boys,*" said Donnie.

Mary Ann bit her lip as she thought it over. Finally she said, "That sounds fair. We shouldn't be prejudiced against you because you're boys." Mary Ann pulled out a spiral notebook and handed it to Donnie. "Put your names and addresses in here. The dues are five dollars each."

Donnie wrote quickly, then passed the book on to the others. After they gave her the money, Mary Ann printed their names onto membership cards. "Here's yours, Spike," she said, handing one to Donnie. "And here are yours, Smasher, Thrasher, Flyboy, and Alvin. Welcome to the club."

"Thanks a lot," said Jonathan. "Where did you get that great block party T-shirt?"

Mary Ann glanced down at her black shirt. "This? I got it yesterday from . . . a . . . somebody," she said nervously.

"Do you think I could buy one?" asked Danny.

"No, they don't have any more. But I heard that these shirts will be for sale at the concert tonight."

Jonathan whispered to Jordan, "These girls could be the ones who took those T-shirts from Casey's."

"But we still don't have any proof," Jonathan answered back softly.

"What are you boys whispering about?" asked Mary Ann. "Is something wrong?"

"We were just talking about the creep that stole Danny's drawing, the one that was to be raffled off at the block party."

Mary Ann's face fell. "Oh, how awful!"

"Do you know who might have done it?" asked Donnie.

"No, we've been here all day," said Mary Ann. "We've been painting banners for tonight." She held one up. The wet paint glistened. It read: NEW KIDS FOREVER!

A short blond girl looked down sadly. "I was hoping to win that picture. I just love Danny."

"Hey, do you know the New Kids?" someone called out. Everyone turned around to see who it was.

Bruno Nadler and the other two Ironheads walked up beside them. "We want to find the New Kids."

"Why do you want to see them?" asked Mary Ann.

"That's our business," said Tim, shaking a drumstick at her. "We just want to talk to them."

"You can go to the concert tonight," said a young girl. "They'll be performing there!"

"Their bodyguards will never let us through," answered Jerry. "If you know where they are, just tell us, okay?"

The girl snapped back, "If you're going to be nasty, I'm not going to tell you anything!"

"So be that way," Tim shouted at her.

"Hey, wait a minute," yelled Donnie. "Everybody lighten up."

"Let's get out of here!" said Tim. "These girls are too stuck-up to talk to us." He turned and started to leave. All of a sudden, his drumstick caught on Joseph's black wig.

The wig flew off!

"You're Joseph McIntyre!" screamed Mary Ann.

Joseph grinned nervously.

She then looked closely at the others. "You're all the New Kids!" she cried. "Right here in Boston Common!"

"The New Kids!" screamed the rest of the Don't Go Girls. "Oh! Yow!"

Jordan held up his finger. *"Shhh!"* But it was too late. Girls from all over the park had heard them screaming and came running from every direction.

The Don't Go Girls went wild. "Jonathan! Jordan! Joseph! Danny! Donnie!" they shouted at once.

"Scatter!" yelled Jordan.

The New Kids took off in five different directions.

Danny shot through the trees at high speed. He was such a fast runner that he reached the edge of the park in no time. When he stopped to catch his breath, he glanced back over his shoulder. The fans were racing toward him, but he had a big lead.

Danny frantically waved both arms and hailed a cab. He hopped in and looked out the back window. A block away he saw Joseph run across the street and down into the subway. Jonathan was right behind him.

On the other side of the park, Donnie was trapped on all sides. He tried to escape but there was no way out. He looked up at a tree overhead to see if he could reach one of the branches. They were too far away, so he bent down as far as he could and leaped into the air. He just missed the branch. When he tried again, he easily caught it. But before he could swing himself up, an eager fan tore off his shoes. Donnie finally broke free and pulled himself to safety. A group of policemen spotted him through the sea of fans. They helped him down and drove him back home.

Jordan ducked and dodged around the crowd, barely avoiding their grasping hands.

He raced for the street, but the stream of traffic was so heavy he couldn't get across. There were no cabs in sight and the fans were closing in.

"Jordan, over here!" someone yelled.

A car pulled up and the door flew open. Calley was driving. Jordan dived inside and Calley took off.

"That was close," he said, out of breath. "Let's get away from here before they catch us."

Calley picked up speed. She pulled in and out of traffic.

"Watch it!" cried Jordan, as she narrowly missed a truck.

Calley quickly spun the wheel and swerved away. She weaved from side to side.

"Take it easy," said Jordan.

Calley turned sharply to the right and screeched around the corner. An empty wine bottle rolled out from under the seat. She tried to kick it back, but she couldn't quite reach it with her foot. She leaned down and frantically felt around the floor.

"Look out!" yelled Jordan.

But his warning was too late. Calley smashed into a telephone pole!

Chapter

9

"JORDAN, ARE YOU OKAY?" cried Calley. "Are you hurt?"

Jordan didn't answer. He was slumped over in his seat. A man ran up to the car and Calley asked him to call 911 right away. He raced over to the pay phone.

Even though Calley was relieved to see that Jordan was still breathing, she panicked when she realized the police would be there any minute. She grabbed the empty wine bottle off the floor, wrapped it in her sweatshirt, and stuffed it into her backpack. She then peeled off three mint lifesavers and quickly chewed them up.

"Jordan, please be all right," she pleaded, tears streaming down her cheeks. "This is all my fault. How could I be so stupid? I'm so sorry. I never meant to hurt you. I never meant to hurt anyone. If I hadn't been drinking, none of this would have happened."

Within seconds, the ambulance pulled up and Calley jumped out of her car. A young man and a woman in white uniforms rushed out to meet her. Calley frantically pointed to Jordan. "I'm okay, but he needs help right away. Please hurry!"

The female paramedic leaned over Jordan and took his pulse. "He's unconscious, but his heart rate and breathing are good," she said.

The male paramedic pulled the stretcher up beside Jordan. The woman put a big foam collar around his neck and the two lifted him up onto the stretcher. They rolled Jordan into the ambulance and Calley climbed in after him.

The siren blared as the vehicle raced across town. Calley thought it seemed like forever before they finally pulled into the hospital's emergency entrance.

Two orderlies ran to meet them. They moved Jordan's motionless body inside the hospital and down the hall. Calley tried to follow him, but a policeman stopped her.

"Were you the driver of the car?" he asked.

She nodded.

"Can you tell me what happened?"

She looked down at the floor. "I was going home from work and . . . I . . . I swerved to miss something and I hit a telephone pole."

"Let me just get a few facts and then you'll get tested."

Her heart stopped. "Tested? What for? I feel fine."

"It's just routine," explained the young doctor sitting behind the desk. "You may have a concussion or internal injuries."

"Oh . . . okay," she reluctantly replied.

The policeman copied down information from Calley's driver's license. "What's your friend's name? We need to contact his family and tell them that he's here."

"Jordan Knight," Calley answered. She gave them his address and phone number.

The policeman lifted his eyebrows. "That name's familiar, but I can't remember why."

Calley sighed. "He's one of the singers in the New Kids on the Block."

The doctor looked concerned. "Half of Boston is going to rush over here the minute they find out he's a patient. I think we'd better put a couple of guards on him. Can you see to it, officer?"

"Right away," the officer replied. He handed Calley back her license and rushed over to the phone.

The doctor told Calley it was time to be X-rayed. He took her into an examining room and gave her a green hospital gown. When she had put it on, he adjusted the X-ray panels in place and left the room.

She felt so lost and scared standing alone in the dark. All she could think about was Jordan. Was he going to be okay? Would he ever speak to her again?

The young doctor returned and examined Calley for internal injuries. He slowly pressed his finger across her stomach. "Is this sore?" he asked.

Calley shook her head. "No, I feel fine."

When he finished checking her over, he told her, "I think you'll probably be okay. But I won't know for sure until I see your X-rays. You can get dressed and sit in the waiting room until they're ready."

"But what about Jordan?" she asked.

"I'll let you know as soon as we get a complete report on his condition."

"Thanks." Calley slowly walked out to the waiting room, her head hung low. Just as she was about to sit down, she saw Joseph come through the front door. He rushed over to her and she burst into tears.

"It's all my fault," she cried.

Joseph put his arm around her shoulders. "It was an accident. It wasn't anybody's fault."

"It *was* my fault. I was drinking." Calley didn't know what made her tell him that. She just blurted it out. But once she did, she felt relieved to have finally told someone her secret.

Joseph didn't answer. He looked shocked.

Calley cried into his shoulder. "I'm so sorry. I'll never forgive myself for what I've done."

Joseph gently patted her head. "Everything will be okay."

The young doctor came out and told Calley that her X-rays were fine and that she could go home. She asked about Jordan and he said his mother and sisters were with him, but there was no news yet.

The doctor left and Calley paced across the floor. "What am I going to do? I can't stop drinking. I've tried. It's ruining my life, and now I may have ruined Jordan's. I may even go to jail!"

"Is that what the police told you?" asked Joseph.

"No, as a matter of fact, they don't know I was drinking. They didn't ask about it or test me for it."

"Then they probably don't know," he said. "I won't tell anyone if you promise to get help."

"Help for what?" asked Donnie as he entered the waiting room.

Calley froze. She didn't want anyone else to know her terrible secret, but something made her tell him. When she explained everything to Donnie, she was surprised that he was as understanding as Joseph had been. He asked her why she started drinking, and more tears rolled down her cheeks.

"I don't know," she said. "I began a few months after my parents were divorced. I'd come home from work and no one would be there, so I'd have a few sips of cooking sherry to make me feel better. Then pretty soon I was sneaking around buying my own bottles of wine. Now I can't get through the day without it. I wish my parents weren't divorced."

Donnie reached over and held her by the

hand. "I know how you feel. My parents got divorced, too. Sometimes the pain was so bad I thought that having a drink or taking drugs would make me feel better. But I didn't try either one."

"Why not?"

"Because I knew they'd only make things worse," he said. "I'd seen too many people get hooked on them and go down the drain."

Donnie lovingly squeezed Calley's hand. "All of us New Kids have had tough lives, but we didn't let it stop us. If we can make it, anyone can. You just have to face things one day at a time. That's the only way to make it through the bad times."

"I don't know," Calley said sadly. "You New Kids have big families to lean on. I have no one and I can't seem to stop drinking, no matter how hard I try. What should I do?"

Joseph gave her a warm smile and told her she would always be part of his family. Then he pointed to the block party flier on the wall. "You can be one of the first to sign up for the Drug and Alcohol Rehabilitation Center at Dorchester Central High. I'm sure they can help you."

"That's a great idea," said Donnie.

"Do you think I can get into the program?" asked Calley.

"We'll talk to them for you," said Joseph.

"Oh, would you? I'd really appreciate it."

"We'd do anything we could to help," Donnie added.

Calley gratefully kissed him on the cheek. "Thanks a lot."

"Hey, don't I get one of those?" Joseph teased her.

"Of course."

Joseph grinned from ear to ear as Calley kissed him too.

"Why don't we go see if there's any news about Jordan?" suggested Donnie.

"Can I come, too?" asked Calley.

"Of course," Donnie replied.

Just at that moment, Sharon Knight rushed over. She was bursting with excitement. "Jordan's going to be okay! The doctor says he can't do much for a day or two. But he'll be fine."

She turned to Calley. "And he was so glad to hear that you weren't hurt."

Calley blushed.

Joseph leaned over and whispered in her ear, "We'll keep your secret. No one else has to know but us."

Calley turned and looked him deep in the eyes. "I won't let you down," she answered confidently. "I promise."

"Do you want to see Jordan now?" asked Sharon.

"Absolutely," Calley replied.

"Here comes Danny," said Joseph.

"Is Jordan okay?" he asked.

"He sure is," Calley said with a sigh of relief.

"Then let's go see him!" declared Donnie.

They headed past the first policeman and down the hall. A second police officer stopped them outside Jordan's room. Sharon said the others were all friends of the family and they went inside.

"Hey, get out of bed, Jordan!" yelled Donnie. "We've got a concert to give."

"Sorry," Jordan replied, with a big wide grin. "I can't make it. You'll have to try to get along without me for a few days."

"No problem," joked Jonathan. "We were thinking of replacing you anyway."

"Who did you have in mind?" he asked.

"I know this chimpanzee who can dance better than you and—"

Jordan threw a pillow at his brother.

Donnie grabbed it before it reached him. "He's back to normal."

"It's really too bad you'll miss the concert tonight," Joseph said to Jordan.

"I know," he replied sadly.

"Maybe he can be there after all," Danny suggested. "Why don't we get an audio/video hookup so he can sing right along with us?"

Jordan's face beamed. "That would be great!"

"I'll call the sound crew. They can arrange everything in no time at all." Danny picked up the phone and began dialing.

The New Kids and their families were all talking and laughing together. Calley suddenly felt out of place. "I'd better go home now," she said, edging toward the door.

Jordan reached over and grabbed her arm. "You're not going anywhere. Somebody's got to keep me company."

"But you have all your family and friends here."

"They'll be leaving pretty soon," he said. "They have to work at the concert tonight. Then I'll be all alone."

"Are you sure you want me to stay?"

"You have to," said Donnie. "You need to be here to stop Jordan from sneaking away and joining us onstage."

117

Calley laughed. "Okay, I'll stay. I'll make sure he doesn't go anywhere."

Jordan grinned. "She's the best-looking bodyguard I ever had."

All of a sudden, someone began shouting in the hallway.

"Maybe our fans found out I was here," said Jordan.

"That sounds more like a fight!" Jonathan replied.

Donnie ran to the door. "It's the Ironheads! They're trying to get past the police guard!"

Chapter
10

JOSEPH, JONATHAN, DANNY, and Donnie raced out into the hall. The Ironheads were shouting at the policeman at the end of the corridor.

"Let us through!" yelled Bruno. "We want to talk to the New Kids."

"It's okay, officer," Donnie told him. "They're our friends."

"We've been looking for you guys everywhere!" said Bruno. "We've tried calling and going by your house, but we couldn't reach anyone."

"What's up?" asked Donnie.

"I came here to tell you who's been impersonating you."

"Who is it?"

"Frankie."

"Frankie who?" Donnie asked. "Do you
mean Frankie Angelino?"

Bruno nodded. "That's your man."

"You're wrong," said Joseph. "Frankie's our
friend."

Danny looked at Bruno suspiciously. "Maybe it was you who did it, and now you're trying
to put the blame on him and throw us off the
track. What about those T-shirts the cops
found at your hideout?"

"They were planted there," said Jerry.

"And the deli food?" asked Joseph. "How
did you get it? Calley said you hadn't been in
Angelino's for a long time."

"We haven't," Bruno replied. "Frankie
brought us all that food when he came over a
few days ago."

Joseph scratched his head. "You listen to
heavy metal records, don't you?"

"Sure we do," said Tim. "But that doesn't
mean we stole any."

"But what about the Don't Go Girls?" Jonathan asked. "They looked pretty suspicious to

me. I thought they might be responsible for everything."

Bruno laughed. "Them? Ha! Frankie worked pretty hard to make them look guilty."

Donnie fingered the peace medallion that hung around his neck. "What makes you think it's Frankie?"

"I was suspicious of him right from the beginning, so I started following him. When I saw him disguise himself and go to Casey's record store, I knew something was up. We tried to tell you about it but we couldn't get you on the phone, so we tried to see you at the radio station. Some cop wouldn't listen and kicked us out of there."

"He sounds like Officer Breen," said Joseph.

"Breen! That was his name," Bruno exclaimed.

"It figures," Joseph replied.

"We were sure it was Frankie when we found those T-shirts in our hideout."

"He may be right," said Danny. "It was Frankie who delivered that deli food. He could have called in the phony order and set it all up himself."

Jonathan agreed that Frankie might be the

impostor. "Jordan told us that Frankie is the one who blamed Mary Ann Lewis for stealing Danny's drawing. He could have been lying about that."

"I still don't get it," said Joseph. "If it is Frankie, why would he do all these things to us? I thought he was our friend."

"He's not trying to hurt you," Bruno explained. "He's angry at us because we wouldn't let him join our band. He came by the other night and asked to be in it again, but now I think it was all a setup to plant the deli food."

"Why would he blame Mary Ann for stealing Danny's picture?" asked Jonathan.

"Because she won't go out with him, and he's really mad at her. He told me."

Donnie thought for a moment. "There's one problem here. Where did the Don't Go Girls get the T-shirts?"

"From Tracey Wahlberg," said Bruno. "Mary Ann told me that she begged Tracey to sell them to her before anyone else had a chance to buy them. Tracey did it only after Mary Ann promised to get all of the Don't Go Girls to volunteer at the new Drug and Alcohol Rehabilitation Center."

"I knew you Ironheads didn't have anything to do with this mess," Donnie told them.

"I'm very sorry I ever thought it was you," Joseph told them.

"Me, too," added Danny and Jonathan.

"Don't worry about it," Bruno replied. "I understand. Frankie planned it so everyone would suspect us."

"I wonder why he didn't plant the stolen records at your hideout, too?" asked Joseph.

"He probably kept them for himself," suggested Tim.

"I bet you're right," said Danny. "We should go find him before he pulls off another one of his stunts."

Bruno pushed his hair out of his eyes. "I think he's working at the deli today. I saw him when I drove by earlier. Why don't I check? I'll call up and ask for Frankie. If he answers, I'll hang up."

"Good idea," said Donnie.

"While he's doing that," Jonathan began, "I'll go tell Jordan and the others that we're leaving."

As Joseph, Danny, and Donnie waited in the lobby with Tim and Jerry, two members of the New Kids' sound crew arrived with the audio/

video equipment. Jonathan returned right after Bruno hung up the phone.

"Mr. Angelino's furious," said Bruno. "He discovered that hundreds of dollars were missing from the cash register. Frankie told him that Calley must have taken it."

Donnie and Bruno looked at each other. "Are you thinking what I'm thinking?" Donnie asked.

Bruno nodded.

"I don't think Calley stole that money," said Donnie. "But I bet I know who did. Come on, guys, let's go find out!"

All seven of them sped off in Bruno's battered old Jeep. They parked it in front of the deli and ran inside.

Frankie was waiting on tables and Mr. Angelino stood behind the counter, angrily chopping up lettuce with a cleaver. "Do you know where Calley is?" yelled the deli owner.

"No," said Bruno.

"When I find her, she's going straight to jail! Officer Breen is out looking for her right this minute."

"Let's hope she doesn't run into him," Joseph said under his breath.

"I don't think Calley stole that money," Donnie told him.

"Yes she did," Frankie replied firmly. "She was the last one to use the cash register before it disappeared. I saw her."

"That's what you say!" yelled Bruno. He stared straight at Frankie as he stepped closer to him.

Frankie edged back.

Donnie and Danny drew in on each side.

"Hey, what's going on?" he protested. "What are you doing?"

Bruno sneered at him. "We just want to make sure you don't go anywhere."

"Why would I go anywhere?"

Bruno couldn't help but laugh. "Listen, wimp, we're on to you. I know you set me up and I'm going to prove it."

All of a sudden, Frankie jumped back and leaped up onto the checkout counter. Danny made a grab for him but he missed. Frankie ran across the counter top and jumped off the end.

Bruno lunged at Frankie but he bolted away. When Mr. Angelino shouted for everyone to stop, Frankie grabbed a salami off the wall. He threw it with all his strength. The salami smashed into Bruno's nose and he doubled over in pain.

Frankie made a break for the door, but

Jonathan jumped out in front of him. Frankie picked up a chair and charged forward. Mr. Angelino yelled even louder.

Donnie grabbed a seltzer bottle from the shelf and shook it up. He twisted off the cap and aimed right for Frankie.

"Yow!" Frankie screamed as he fell backward. He struggled to keep his balance, but he lost control and toppled into the ice cream machine. He hit the handle as he fell to the floor and strawberry soft serve poured down over his head.

Danny and Donnie grabbed Frankie by the legs and turned him upside down. They shook him until money poured out of his pockets.

Donnie pointed to the hundreds of dollars on the floor. "Frankie took the money out of the cash register. Not Calley."

"You can't prove that," Frankie whined.

"Oh, yes I can," said Mr. Angelino. "The stolen bills were brand new from the bank this morning. They sent me the serial numbers as soon as I reported they were gone." He pulled the list out of his pocket and compared it to the money. "It was you. Why would you do this?"

"It's none of your business."

"Well, it's *my* business," said Joseph.

"Calley's my friend and I want to know why you framed her."

"That's a stupid question," he said. "I framed her so no one would know I took the money."

"What were you going to do with it?" Bruno asked angrily.

"I was going to buy fireworks, so I could get you in big trouble this time! I planned to set off the fireworks in the middle of the New Kids concert. I had it all fixed so you Ironheads would be blamed. I ordered that deli food, and took those heavy metal records, and the New Kids T-shirts, just to make sure everyone would believe you did it."

Tim raised his fist. "You slimy little dirtbag."

"What's going on here?" bellowed Officer Breen as he came through the door.

"I never thought I'd be glad to see that guy," Joseph joked to Danny.

"Take him away, officer," said Mr. Angelino. "Frankie's responsible for all these crimes against the New Kids. It wasn't Calley and it wasn't a publicity stunt either."

"Oh . . . ah . . . I see," he stammered.

Danny and Joseph chuckled.

Officer Breen grabbed Frankie by the arm. "Let's go down to headquarters, young man."

When he led Frankie to the door, Jonathan yelled out, "Hey, where's Danny's picture?"

"Over there," Frankie said. He pointed to the storage room. "It's behind the stack of paper towels."

Jonathan opened the door and found it right away. "Look," he said, holding it up for everyone to see. "It's not damaged. We can still use it in the block party raffle tonight."

"The block party!" cried Donnie. "I almost forgot. We have to get over to the high school right away. Our concert is in less than half an hour!"

"I'll drive you there," said Bruno.

They all piled into his Jeep and took off. The neighborhood streets were packed full of people walking, driving, and bicycling to the concert. The Jeep got stuck in traffic because there were so many people everywhere.

Jonathan grew more nervous with every passing second. "We won't get there in time."

"Sure you will," Bruno replied. "Just watch." He twisted the steering wheel to the left and immediately drove off in the opposite direction.

"Where are we going?" asked Donnie.

Bruno darted around the corner. "We're taking the back way. These side streets will lead us around to the rear entrance of the school faster than if we try to go in the front."

"Good plan!" Donnie told him.

In no time at all, they arrived behind Dorchester Central High School.

Dick Scott's car was parked right next to the building. The New Kids rushed out and pounded on the door to the gym. Dick pushed it open. "There you are! Jordan said you left the hospital a long time ago. Where have you been?"

"We'll tell you about it later," said Donnie. "Where do we go to get ready?"

Dick pointed to the locker room. "The stage out front is all set. We have an audio/video hook-up to the hospital and Jordan is waiting to join in."

The New Kids headed inside the gym, but when the Ironheads didn't follow them, Donnie yelled to Bruno, "Why don't you come backstage with us?"

"Maybe next time," said Bruno. He reached for the fire escape ladder that led to the roof. "We'll watch the show from up top. That's the best seat in the house."

"Great!" cheered Donnie. "See you there."

The Ironheads scrambled up the ladder and the New Kids hurried to get ready. Their families were all jammed into the locker room, waiting for them to arrive.

"That was a close one," exclaimed Tracey Wahlberg, giving her brother Donnie a big hug.

"I knew they'd get here," Joseph's dad said confidently.

Melissa Wood smiled. "They always do!"

It took only a few minutes for the singers to get into their concert clothes and be ready for the show. Joseph pulled on a big Boston Red Sox T-shirt over his black jeans. Donnie threw on two more peace sign medallions. They hung down over his faded blue overalls. Jonathan and Danny both wore black hats and blue jeans. Jonathan added a bright multicolored vest on top of his white T-shirt.

Tracey gave one of the block party T-shirts to Danny and he put it on. "We sold every last ticket to the show," she said. "And all of the T-shirts."

"The money's going to a great cause," added Mr. McIntyre. "The Drug and Alcohol Rehabilitation Center is going to help a lot of people get out of trouble."

Donnie and Joseph looked over at each other and smiled about Calley. They were both happy to know that she would soon get the help she needed.

Melissa announced that it was time to go. She led the New Kids down the hall to the edge of the stage. A giant platform had been built in front of the school. Three city blocks had been roped off and the streets were jammed with screaming fans of all ages.

Dick Scott called everyone into the huddle, including the New Kids' families. They had a moment of silence, then everyone broke into a cheer: "NEW KIDS ROCK THE BLOCK! NEW KIDS ROCK THE BLOCK!"

Danny, Donnie, Jonathan, and Joseph burst out on stage and the crowd went wild. Jordan waved from the large video screen overhead and the fans yelled even louder.

Donnie stepped forward to lead the first song. "I want to dedicate this concert to the whole neighborhood! We're all here to make it a better place."

"Yeah!" shouted every last person, including the Ironheads, looking down from the roof above. When Donnie started the song, he spotted the Don't Go Girls lined up at the edge of the stage.

He threw them a kiss.

NEW BOOKS FROM
BOXTREE

Boxtree

HOME AND AWAY™

Dangerous Ride
By Sally Darroll

Carly and her friends had been warned
about the dangers of hitch-hiking but she
had refused to listen . . .

ISBN: 1–85283–073–5

Family Matters
By Mark Butler

Roo's jealous scheming has already ruined
her father's marriage. Now, hopelessly in
love with Frank, but expecting Brett's
baby, she is bent on making everybody's
life a misery.

ISBN: 1–85283–074–3

The Unofficial
HOW TO BEAT NINTENDO®

By Jon Sutherland & Nigel Gross

Read this book and become a Nintendo®
video game ace. Whether you are a
beginner or an experienced campaigner,
HOW TO BEAT NINTENDO® will help
you solve the mysteries of over 140 of the
most popular games.

Each game is given a brief, accurate
description and a rating. You are given the
winning strategies you will need and
essential tips to help you win.

ISBN: 1–85283–075–1